Bell Farm

With Best Wishes

Mollie Barneby.

Bell Farm

M. L. BARNEBY

Published by M.L. Barneby
Copyright © M. L. Barneby, 2002
Illustrations copyright © Rosanna Shakerley, 2002

ISBN 0 9544322 0 7

Cover and text designed by Nicky Barneby

Typeset in 10.75/15pt Trump Mediaeval
Printed and bound by Four Way Print Ltd, Saltash, Cornwall

Dedicated to my four children and eight grandchildren.

Special thanks to my grandson John Barneby who inspired me to finish this book, to my daughter Rosanna Shakerley for the beautiful illustrations, and to my grand daughter Nicky Barneby without whom this story would never have been made into a book.

CHAPTER ONE
The Funeral

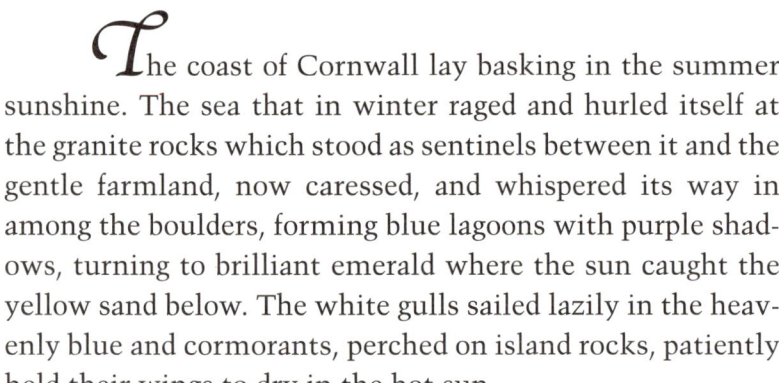

*T*he coast of Cornwall lay basking in the summer sunshine. The sea that in winter raged and hurled itself at the granite rocks which stood as sentinels between it and the gentle farmland, now caressed, and whispered its way in among the boulders, forming blue lagoons with purple shadows, turning to brilliant emerald where the sun caught the yellow sand below. The white gulls sailed lazily in the heavenly blue and cormorants, perched on island rocks, patiently held their wings to dry in the hot sun.

A rough track ran between two fields leading from Bell Farm to the cove. In winter when the gales brought in the seaweed, the farm men used this track to fetch it up in cart loads, mixed with dung it made good manure for the land. Now, the track was overgrown, with blue bells and red campion stitchwort like little stars and tall green ferns. The black birds sang in the privacy of the sloe trees and distant larks twittered high above the granite carn.

The farmhouse was E-shaped, facing south west, a jutting wing on either side, to keep out the worst of the north and east gales.

Outside the front door there was a small garden surrounded by a stone wall, a slate slab path ran between two plots of grass to the wicket gate. Round the edges the borders were gay with summer flowers. Scented pinks, snapdragons, marigolds and hollyhocks, pink and cream, standing like soldiers against the weather beaten granite of the house.

Across the yard outside the wall, was the great barn, where the wagons, carts and farm implements were kept. Huge coils of rope for the hay and harvest wagons hung on the walls among the pikes, heavels and pitchforks. Up above, was the granary, at one end of which hung the rope that pulled the bell from which the farm got its name Bell Farm. A tower had been built on one end of the roof, housing a huge bell, which was used to give warning when a wreck came in or a ship was in distress.

It was a small manor and had been the home of the Kerris' family for two hundred years. Now, the old house lay almost silent in the hot sunshine, it had witnessed many births and deaths, joys and tragedies so that another one seemed to make little difference. The sun beat down on the old slate roof and the long latticed windows blinked and waited.

In the dining room Richard Kerris lay in his coffin waiting for his funeral – maybe his soul waited also and listened, as the grandfather clock with its flower painted face ticked away the minutes.

Upstairs in her bedroom Sara sat at the open window

gazing unseeingly out at the calm sea. She was dressed in black – a widows veil hid her face and every now and then she lifted a corner to wipe away the silent tears that trickled down her face. She couldn't believe that her Richard was no more. She would never forget the scene that had met her eyes as she walked over the pale short grass of the new mown hay field, only three days before.

They were taking down a large dead tree in the middle of the zawn meadow before it was ploughed up. She had stood and watched, a basket of saffron buns wrapped in a clean cloth over one arm and a jug of tea in her other hand.

In the middle of the field two men stood by their axes resting, while four others and Richard encouraged a sweating team of horses as they strained at the long chains harnessed behind them to the tree. The tree had groaned and creaked as it began to sway – the chains ease off and one had got caught round a boulder – Richard ran forward to free it – at the release the horses lurched forward – the tree swayed – hung momentarily suspended – then crashed to earth taking Richard with it. Sara had been rooted to the spot with horror. Recovering, she had raced across the remaining field. The men hacked and sawed at the branches, at last they managed to clear a way to Richard and were able to pull him clear – he had lain limp and still, the blood oozed, and congealed from an ugly wound on the back of his head, the men gently turned him over, Sara had knelt on the grass beside him, taken his head between her hands and begged him to speak to her. 'Richard, Richard speak to me, speak to me', she had cried. As she had let go of his head, it had fallen back onto the grass, she had flung herself across his chest beseeching him. Old Joby, one of the ageing men who had served Richard's father, had come forward and lifted her, led her back to the house. Richard himself, had been felled by the giant tree.

Sara remembered there was an old saying, that a tree will get its own back. Her tears flowed afresh, as she relived the scene. She clenched her fists and tightened every muscle in her face in an effort to stem them. She held her breath, fighting for self control. She could not, would not go to Church without some semblance of composure.

Downstairs, relatives and friends were gathering in the parlour. It smelt fusty, the windows were shut and curtains drawn, as was the custom in a bereaved house. Everyone wore black and talked among themselves in whispers. Discussing the tragedy and wondering what would happen to the farm with only two women to look after it.

In the kitchen, Sara and Richard's only child, Martha was preparing the ham tea which was customary after a funeral, she was of medium height with softly waving brown hair and the bluest of blue eyes. At this moment she looked very small and lonesome, a mere child despite her twenty years and black dress. She cast a last look at the long scrubbed table covered with a white cloth, laid out with a huge home cured ham, large plates of bread and butter, two glass pots of mustard, dishes of homemade jam and clotted cream, fresh baked scones, saffron buns and crowning all in the middle of the table a huge black cake, smelling of spice and cinnamon, with coarse white sugar sprinkled on the top. The windows were shuttered, the curtains drawn, the smell of baking heavy in the air. The fire roared and flamed in the great black

Cornish slab with its shining brass knobs. Shep, Richard's devoted black and white mongrel sheep dog, who had been his shadow ever since she was a pup, lay dejected in her basket, her head on her paws, her eyes turned up showing the whites. Martha looked down, meeting whose questioning eyes, she stooped, knelt on the floor beside the basket, held Shep's head close against her, wetting it with tears.

'Oh! Shep, Shep', she sobbed, 'whatever shall we do?' Shep tried to be a comfort, licking the tears off her face and whimpered, as if she would speak.

There was a sound outside of horses hooves and crunching gravel. Martha got up, blew her nose, and lifting a corner of the curtain peeped out. Oh dear, it was time to go, the undertaker had arrived – she smoothed her hair with her hands and reached for a new hat of black straw that lay on a chair, arranged it on her head with the aid of a faded mirror. This then was the moment, the final moment – they would now take the last of the Kerris' from Bell Farm to his resting place.

There was a knock on the front door, Martha opened it – Mr Treneer stood diffidently on the doorstep, wearing his black frock coat, his tall hat and black gloves in his hand. He was a long thin man with a weather beaten face. A mass of hoary grey hair and bushy side whiskers, his eyes were deep set under shaggy brows and very penetrating. He was the local carpenter and undertaker, as was his father before him. His coat green with age, had probably been handed down from father to son. Martha invited him in. Carefully wiping his shiny black boots on the mat, he followed her through the flower filled hall to the dining room. They spoke together in undertones.

'Neew Miss Kerris, yew leave everything to me,' he whispered. 'Be all the mourners here yet?'

'I think so, I'll go and see a minute,' she said.

While Martha was out of the room, Mr Treneer looked about him. The room was low and square with a long latticed window matching the one in the parlour, on the other side of the hall. There was a heavy Georgian side board covered with such things as a cake stand, biscuit barrel, cut glass pickle jar, plated cruet stand and a wine coaster, wedding presents he supposed. Over the centre of the mantelpiece there hung a framed illuminated text, 'God helps those who help themselves,' he read. Well Richard Kerris had certainly done that he thought. The dining table was also heavy Georgian mahogany with round bulbous legs, it was covered with a red plush cloth and on this the coffin rested. The grandfather clock with its painted face struck the half after two, Mr Treneer took his gold time piece from his waistcoat pocket and checked the time – the funeral was at three o'clock, plenty of time, he thought.

Martha came back into the room, he raised his shaggy eyebrows at her questioningly.

'Yes' she said in a loud whisper, 'they are all here.'

Mr Treneer felt sorry for her. She looked such a child, and so pathetic in her new black dress. He ventured to put his hand gently on her shoulder.

'You look after your Mother, I'll call you when us are ready to start. Do you think us needs to take the waggonette to Church – or would you rather walk?'

'I think it would be nicer to walk,' she said.

'Right then, you go to your Mother, I'll call 'ee in a minute.'

The farm workers were to be the bearers, they waited in the barn beside the harvest wagon dressed in their dark Sunday suits. The two best farm horses were harnessed up. In front Lady a dark brown bay shining like silk, behind her Prince, a powerful dapple grey. Black ribbons had been plaited into their manes and tails. George Pearce the head horseman stood up on the front of the wagon. The arrival of Mr Treneer and his men was the signal for them to move round to the front door. The harness brasses glinted in the sun and jingled as they moved. The farm workers formed a procession in front, as they arrived at the front door old George pulled gently on the long reins.

'Whoa there my beauties, whoa there,' he crooned. The horses twitched their ears and flicked their tails, understanding every inflection in his voice.

Mr Treneer motioned the bearers into the dining room, where they took up the heavy coffin. Richard Kerris had been a big man. They strained every muscle and the veins stood out on their necks as they edged their way past the flowers in the hall. Mr Treneer's men collected the wreaths, crosses and sheaths of flowers. When the coffin was in place on the wagon they covered it completely.

Martha quietly lifted the latch of the door to her Mother's room and went in. Sara was lost in her troubles, she didn't hear her and jumped when Martha gently touched her shoulder.

'Mr Treneer is here Mother,' she said, then knelt down and slipped her arm round Sara's shoulders holding her close, their heads together. 'Come now 'tis time to go to the Church,' she whispered. Sara stared at Martha with far away unseeing eyes and got stiffly to her feet, still clutching her handkerchief. She seemed to have been waiting for hours, her limbs would hardly move. Martha realised that she would have to be her Mother's strength. She felt heart broken. Her Mother seemed to have shrunk and grown old in a few days. She took her arm, led her across the room and down the stairs. The coffin was already on the harvest wagon, almost hidden under the mountain of flowers. The horses whisked their tails and tossed their manes, the black ribbons bobbed incongruously in the June sunshine. The farm men stood waiting on either side – relatives and close friends were gathered a little way behind to leave room for Sara and Martha. As they came out of the dim interior into the bright sunshine and flower filled garden, Sara was almost blinded by the strong light. She stopped and hesitated, but Martha's strong arm propelled her slowly forward to take their place behind the wagon.

Mr Treneer nodded to old George who flicked the reins and clicked his tongue to Lady and Prince. They, obedient to his command, moved forward across the yard and out into the village where a sight met their eyes. Friends, neighbours and villagers, all men, lined the street all the way to the Church and bent their heads in silent respect.

Kerris men had been loved and respected for generations. Taking the lead in all local affairs, always ready with advice or help in kind, no one had ever been turned empty away from Bell Farm, while a Kerris had lived there. Richard had been no exception to the rule. Tall, bronzed, weather beaten, strong as an ox, taking always the hardest work and heaviest burden for himself. Here, men who had received seed for their planting, help with their tilling, haymaking, or harvest, thought on these things as the sad little procession passed on its way.

At the other end of the village, the Parson waited at the Church gate in his white surplus his hands folded in front of him.

Inside, the old Church was cool and dim, there was a fragrance of wax and summer flowers in the air from the candles and vases arranged with loving care on the altar. Miss Jago, the school mistress, sat waiting at the organ, when she heard the approach of the mourners she lifted her hands and began very softly to play.

Martha guided Sara into a front pew and sat down beside her. She gave a gentle sigh of relief, the first stage of this nightmare over. The other members of the small procession settled themselves into pews behind them. The bearers came struggling in with their heavy burden, followed by the men from the street, coughing nervously, shuffling their feet and bending forward in their pews in an attitude of prayer.

The Parson took his place – everybody stood up – the service began – his clear voice rose and fell as he read the service – the men at the back made the responses. Sara sat clasping Martha's hand, her mind far removed from those around her and that which was taking place. She was in the zawn meadow – the seagulls crying and bees humming as she walked with her tea basket between the flower filled hedges, the smell of the new mown hay in her nostrils. The murmur of the sea on the rocks below the meadow, and the murmur of the Parson's voice, were all one to her – everybody stood up, the organ played and the full-throated voices of many men were uplifted in song – she saw the face of Jesus in the stained-glass window, his hands uplifted in an attitude of blessing, a cloud beneath his feet a halo round his head and behind him a background of soft deep blue – his face was the face of Richard, he seemed to smile.

Sara gave a start as Martha touched her arm.

'Come Mother,' she whispered.

The bearers came forward, raised the heavy coffin and bore it away. Martha took her arm and guided her into the church yard. The sky had become overcast and a light breeze wafted Parson's surplus as he led them to the grave – Martha thought it seemed so small to be the resting place of her tall strong Father. Sara couldn't feel that he was there at all – she lifted her face to the sky – the clouds were growing thicker and moving faster as the breeze grew stronger. Her spirit went to meet his soul in the zawn meadow and away beyond the infinite space of the sea.

'Earth to earth, ashes to ashes, dust to dust,' murmured the Parson. Far away Sara heard a seagull cry.

Back at the farm again, relatives and friends crowded into the warmth and comfort of the old house, murmuring and twittering like chickens under a broody hen. Tea was ready. Sam, old George's grandson, and Janie his sister, who had been helping in the house for two years, stood by the stove that took up almost the entire wall at the far end of the kitchen and handled the big black iron kettles that bubbled and hissed as they boiled. Janie held first a big china tea pot with roses on it and then a big earthenware one that was used to make croust for the men in the field, while Sam poured the boiling water on to the tea.

Aunty Mary left her coat in the back room and came

bustling in to help. She was plump and rosy, with bright beady eyes always a twinkle. She wore her best dress, the bodice now a little tight, embroidered all over with jet beads. As she entered the kitchen Joel Kerris, Richard's cousin put his great hand on her shoulder.

''Ow are 'ee Meery m'dear' he bellowed. Aunty Mary turned.

'Oh! 'tis yeew me 'ansom,' she bridled up at him, 'I'm very well in me self, an' yeew?'

'Oh, I'm hearty enough me dear, but 'ow is Sara? They bin telling me as 'ow she'm very slight, very slight!'

''Ees, poor soul – but then 'tis only what we'd expect ain't it? She'll come about again when this 'eer funeral is past won't she?'

''Ees, s'pose, but 'tis some wisht job, some wisht job Meery,' Joel regarded his boots for a moment and shook his head, 'Ah well, that's where's to! Me dear,' and with that parting remark he took himself off to join the press of folks in the parlour.

Aunt Mary bustled into the kitchen. Joel's boy Jack was cutting up the ham and filling plates as fast as he could.

'Now Janie, give us the teapot, yeew take up the tray an' ca' that there tea rewnd. Sam! Ketch up a tray an' ca' they plates of ham into the parlour, take the mustard with yeew mind, come back for the bread and butter!'

Aunt Mary went on pouring cups of tea. It was very hot in the kitchen, her face was puce and she perspired profusely but she was glad to have something to do. Presently Martha joined her.

'Oh there yeew are me dear, I was wondering where yeew

was to,' she put down the heavy teapot and looked at Martha.

Martha had been upstairs with her Mother and to take her hat off. She had never been to a funeral before, the experience had upset her. After settling Sara, she had sought the privacy of her own room for a moment, suddenly the reaction of the strain of the last few days had overwhelmed her. She sat on a chair, leant her aching head against the old chest of drawers, as though it were a friend, and wept.

Aunt Mary noticed at once that she had been crying, so thought to occupy her.

''Tis some hot in 'ere dear, will yeew take over this 'ere teapot for a minute? I'll go in the parlour an see 'ow many more d'want tea,' Martha took up the teapot, her throat was aching as she tried to suppress the tears. Jack finished cutting the ham, he turned and saw her dripping tears into the teacups. He went over and put his arm round her shoulders.

'There there, don't 'ee go for to cry now,' he whispered to her, 'Go on in the parlour and sit dewn a minute, I'll bring 'ee a cup o tea, go on now,' he said and gave her a gentle push towards the parlour door.

Martha hoped to slip into the room unnoticed, but this she soon realised was impossible – she was converged upon from every side, friends and relatives overwhelmed her, her head swam, the heat was oppressive, suddenly she caught sight of Aunt Mary sitting on a chair against the wall, wiping her face over with a handkerchief. Here was a way of escape. She eased her way across the room and joined her.

''Tis some 'ot in 'ere Martha dear, could us ave the window open a bit do 'ee think?' she said, still mopping her brow. Martha made her way along to the latticed window and flung it wide. Lingered, holding her hot face to the cooling breeze that came from the rising wind, ruffling her hair and billowing the curtains out into the room.

Sam and Janie hurried to and fro, to and fro, with their trays of food and steaming cups of tea, everyone ate their fill. The talk rose and fell, the matter was threshed out over and over again. Everyone was wise, as everyone is, after the event.

At last, the day was over. Martha bolted the doors, knelt and kissed Shep who lay wistful, not quite understanding, in her basket.

'Good night dear Shep,' she whispered. Then straightening herself, she went to the table and turned the lamp down, looked around at the dear familiar things. It felt warm and safe, the coals settled in the grate. She lit her candle, blew the lamp out and slowly mounted the old stairs, the house felt strangely empty and silent. Richard Kerris had filled his home, his women folk had lived for him. Sara lay in bed, her hair like a cloud on the pillow, her face turned to the open window.

'Good night Mother,' Martha whispered. Sara turned and held her arm out to her. Martha put down the candle, went to the bed and laid her head beside Sara's on the pillow. So for a moment they clung together in silent understanding. Sara looked at the little face, the tumbled hair, all her Mother love and protective instinct was aroused. Tomorrow I will see to everything. I must keep a roof over our heads. She kissed the head in the crook of her arm, Martha stirred.

'Time to go to bed dear,' Sara whispered.

Alone again, Sara got out of bed – went to the window –

leant her arms on the window ledge and gazed across the dusky meadows to the dark smudge that was the sea. She wore a white cambric nightgown, her long hair falling like a cloak around her shoulders. There was no moon, the wind had risen but the air was soft and sweet with a tang of salt in it. The fresh breeze caressed and blew her hair about her face – she prayed for strength – tried to feel Richard near – surely his spirit could not be so far away? In the distance a curlew called, once, and then again, how could she ever bear it? She held her face to the cool night air – felt raindrops mingle with her tears. Far away – below the zawn meadow, the sea whispered to her, as it communed with the indigo rocks –

Shush – shush – shush.

CHAPTER TWO

John Trethewey

The hot African sun beat down on the bowed head of John Trethewey as he stood, his hat held against his chest – alone beside the grave of his Mother – the funeral had taken place three weeks before – the flowers now faded and dead – the soil burnt dry and yellow on the little mound. He brought a stout wooden cross with him and a mallet and hammered it firmly into the ground at the head of the grave. The simple inscription read, 'Here lies Gwendolin Trethewey, beside her husband Benjamin Trethewey – daughter of John Eade of Pentewan, Cornwall, England. In loving memory – John, their son,' This was the last thing that John could do for his parents. His mind was now made up – he would return to Cornwall the home of his people, buy a farm and settle there. He blew a kiss – said goodbye and replaced his hat and left.

John's father, Benjamin was a second son, so he had turned

to mining, while his elder brother inherited the family farm. But people from England not born to the hot climate died early in Africa and so it had been with his parents – he had no brothers or sisters and was only thirty, but his father had left him in comfortable circumstances. Looking through the old family albums at the faded photographs of the farm in Cornwall, the sea, the rugged cliffs, fisher folk, their boats and nets – fish being landed in great baskets that spilled out on to the harbour side. All the things that went to make up the life his parents had left behind, when they emigrated to a small mining town in the middle of nowhere in Africa. He was going to sell the house, with its tin roof, spacious veranda and shady garden, where his mother used to sit under a big tree and sew or knit, and return to England and most of all, Cornwall, where he would buy a farm of his own, settle and make a home.

John had written some months ago to his cousin James, who farmed near Lansallo in Cornwall telling him of his father's death and his mother's illness, so he was not altogether surprised to receive a letter with an English stamp. The letter was from James, expressing in simple words, the sorrow he and his wife Amy felt for him, at the loss of both his father and mother in a relatively short space of time. He went on to say that 'Now you have lost both your parents, I imagine there is nothing much to keep you. Why don't you come to Cornwall?' Yes! That was what his cousin said, and that was what he intended to do.

There then followed a couple of weeks sorting, selling and packing. It was easy enough to sell the homestead, it was a tidy little place with a pretty garden that his mother had made. When all was settled John said his goodbyes and was on his way.

As the steamer made its way up the English Channel towards Plymouth, John stood on deck leaning against the rail. He was tall, over six foot in his socks and broad with it. His hair was thick and dark and curled at his temples, as he turned to face the wind and damp misty air. His features were handsome and regular but tanned and swarthy from the life he had led.

The sea gulls filled the sky crying and wheeling overhead as if in welcome – a strange thrill went through his whole body – his thoughts and emotions reached out towards his homeland. He braced himself against the rails, his hands and knuckles white with cold and tense excitement. There it was – the grey shadow showing through the mist, the coast of Cornwall. He could just discern the white surf breaking on the rocky shoreline.

Plymouth was cold and grey, but the quayside was a bustle with meetings, greetings, laughter and tears – carts and wagons of all descriptions. John shouldered his bags that held what few possessions he had brought with him and made his way through the throngs of people to look for a likely Inn. Darkness was falling and if he put up for the night he could find out in the morning about an attorney to advise him on such matters as banking and how best to set about his journey to Cornwall in search of a farm.

After rejecting several small and rather down at heels or noisy houses, he came upon a solid stone building with a beautiful painted sign of 'The Dolphin' hanging outside and decided it looked a likely sort of place to try his luck. There was a small courtyard in front with a gate and a path that led up to the open door, where a welcoming light streamed out. Inside it was all warmth and comfort, a large square taproom – a big open fire place, a blazing log fire, with an iron kettle suspended from a hook boiling over and hissing on to the logs. He dropped his bags and banged on the table with his fist – almost at once a door at the back opened and young Mrs Jenkin came hurrying out – she was round and rosy with dark frizzy hair parted in the middle and twisted up into a knot at the back of her head. She wore a blue blouse, buttoned to the neck, a long dark skirt and was wiping her hands on a blue check apron as she came.

"Ullo Sir' Just off the boat are 'ee? I s'pose you're wanting a bed for th'night?' she said with a broad smile.

'Yes,' said John, 'I shall be very glad if you can let me have a room for the night, I should also like some hot water and dinner later – if you can manage all that.'

'Oh 'ess Sir, we're used to they what comes off the boat – you follow me 'an I'll show you to your room.' Off she went through the door at the back again and up a quite wide dark oak stair with a beautifully carved rail and polished treads – the passage above was wide and the polished boards reflected the dim light. Mrs Jenkin led the way carrying a thick tall candle and ushered him into a room at the end. It had massive beams, a lattice window, with a window seat that overlooked the harbour where the masts and lights of the ships reflected in the water. The bed was broad and had a panelled oak headboard and two oak stumps each side of the foot – it looked as if it had once been a four-poster, cut down. The chintzes were rosy and gay – there was an oak press to hang his clothes, a chest of drawers and a wash stand with a china jug and basin. A fire was laid on the ash in the hearth and Mrs Jenkin took a paper spill, lighted it at the candle, stooped and set the fire alight – the flames leaped up and filled the whole room with light and warmth. John laughed aloud and rubbed his hands with delight.

'This is what I really call a home coming,' he said.

'Do you belong in these parts then?' she said.

'No, but my parents came from Cornwall and went to Africa mining, my cousin lives in Cornwall on my grandfather's farm; I am going down there to buy a farm and settle myself.'

'Oh,' she said, 'so you ha' come all the way from Africa? My! Well, you must be some 'ungry?! She laughed, her cheeks shone and her dark eyes danced reflecting back the candle light. 'You make yourself comfortable,' she said, 'There's water in the jug for you to wash your hands.' And with that she left him and softly closed the door.

John looked about him. Here was real English comfort. Outside he could hear the carts thundering along over the cobbles of the wet dark street. Inside this room there was candle light and fire light, a warm carpet beneath his feet, curtains with flowers all over them, at the windows, shutting out the night.

He took off his coat – heavy against the cold and damp, opened his bag and took out a light velvet one – he fingered it lovingly – his Mother's last birthday present to him and made by her small capable hands. He held it for a minute against his cheek, hoping a little of her perfume would still be clinging to it. There was no perfume only the smell of his polished boots that had been in the same bag. He shook out the folds and some pieces of old faded tissue paper fell to the floor. He hung it over a chair beside the washstand, poured some water from the jug into the bowl and washed his hands. The soap had a faint scent and he liked it. A white linen hand towel lay beside the bowl. He took it up – it felt soft and silky between his fingers. He had not been used to such luxury. He took his velvet coat from the chair, shrugged himself into it, drew the armchair nearer to the fire and sat down, stretching his long legs and his feet to the warmth of the blaze on the hearth. He closed his eyes, felt wrapped around with happy contentment, thinking to himself if this is England, then I have certainly made the right decision to come home.

He must have dozed off for an hour. He woke up with a start to the sound of hearty laughter and loud voices. The logs on the hearth had burnt low, he stretched, yawned, ran his fingers through his hair and sat up. The tap room must be full of people by now, he suddenly realised how hungry he was. Getting to his feat, he kicked the logs to a blaze, went to the wash stand and poured some fresh water, sluiced his face with his hands and ran his wet fingers through his hair, took the linen towel, rubbed his face vigorously and dried his hands. This done, he emptied the contents of his travelling pack onto the bed. A nightshirt – he put on the pillows, found his toilet pack, shaving tackle, a shaving mirror, toothbrush and lastly put a comb through his hair, gave his coat a shrug and looking at his reflection in the mirror decided his appearance was well enough for him to go downstairs and order his dinner.

The tap room was crowded and hazy with smoke, warm

and pleasantly full of the smell of wood smoke and warm humanity. Going to the bar he ordered a pint of bitter ale – took the tankard and looked around for a table. They all seemed to be occupied, but he spied one in the corner with only one occupant, a sober looking fellow in a dark suit. John went over and introduced himself, 'John Trethewey', nice to meet you – mind if I sit here?'

The man smiled, 'No not at all, sit down man, sit down by all means.' He held out his hand across the table. 'George Trescawn, attorney – glad to meet you too – from your speech, I guess you are not from these parts?'

'No, as a matter of fact, I arrived from Africa on the steamer this very evening.' At that moment Mrs Jenkin appeared interrupting their conversation to ask John what he would like for his dinner – there was a bowl of soup, a dish of kidneys and a leg of boiled mutton to follow, with onions, Swedes and potatoes in their skins. After his long journey and the ships food, this sounded wonderful, he rubbed his hands together in pleasurable anticipation.

'Yes, thank you Mrs Jenkin, I'll take the lot!' he laughed at her and she thought 'My, he's some 'ansom and no mistake'. She blushed at her own thoughts, and hurried off to get his food.

George Trescawn prompted him, 'You were just telling me you have arrived today, all the way from Africa?'

'Ah, yes, that's right. I was born out there of Cornish parents, mining you know. My father was a second son, my cousin has a bigish farm in Cornwall, at a place called Lanethra, a nice house he's got there – stone, stone mullioned windows, of course I've only seen a faded photograph, but it looks good to me. I'm planning to see a banker tomorrow, then find an attorney to help and advise me how to set about buying a farm myself. I plan to settle in Cornwall, go into farming – eventually get married and settle there.'

George looked up, interested. 'Maybe I could be of use to you,' he said. 'I deal with a lot of property business.' Mrs Jenkin reappeared carrying a loaded tray – she was flushed by her exertions. 'There now, there's your soup, some crusty bread, here are the kidneys,' she lifted the lid of a plated dish. 'Got hot water underneath – they'll stay 'ot while you eat your soup,' she unloaded the tray, and disappeared through the door at the back again. George Trescawn got up and moved to go 'I'm going home to my dinner,' he said, 'My Missus will be waiting for me.' He felt in his waist coat pocket, took out a small leather case and extracted a card which he held out to John – 'Here's my card,' he said, 'I shall be only too glad if I can help you in anyway.' John took the card in his left hand, held out his right hand and they gave a hearty handshake which was to cement their friendship for many years to come.

John attacked his soup – it was mutton broth – made from the stock the leg had been cooked in, he thought. It tasted good, he broke the bread and dipped pieces into it – sucking the liquid and scrunching the crisp crust. He lifted the tankard and had a swill of his ale, then lifted the lid from the kidneys – they smelled and looked good – mushrooms from the fields and brown gravy around them. John ate with relish, dipping the last of the bread and sopping up the gravy. He wiped his mouth with the white napkin provided, took up his tankard, lent back in his chair and took stock of the rest of the company. While he waited for his mutton – he listened to snatches of the conversation around him.

A man, a farming type, who sat at the next table, was voicing his opinion in a loud voice. What John heard of his conversation made him listen attentively.

'Some wisht job about that there Richard Kerris 'edna – felled by 'is own tree and no mistake – knocked 'im flat, dead as a door nail when they got 'im out from under – 'tis five months now, since they 'ad the funeral – fine funeral and no mistake – 'ess I went down there for it. Two women down there by themselves, but it won't do – I said to my Missus – 'Winnie', I said 'they two women they ain't got no son – only 'ad one daughter and she be not much more than a child – eighteen years of age – they do tell me. Pretty little maid. I seen 'er at the funeral – she'm more than pretty really – like her Mother Sara and she come from the Manor. Oh – some talk when Richard Kerris married Sara from the Manor – that was some weddin' that was – and took 'er 'ome to Bell Farm'. Now there's a place for you – that's some farm I call it, some farm – she'll 'ave to sell – it will come on the market, you mark my words.' And so he rambled on.

John was so intrigued he hardly noticed the boiled mutton arriving and he ate it in a dream. The edge was off his appetite anyway. Bell Farm he said to himself – Bell Farm will have to come on the market – only two women there and they will have to sell.' He felt in his pocket for George Trescawn's card and wrote on the back Bell Farm in large black letters – he felt strange, as if a hand had been laid on his shoulder and the name whispering in his ears, Bell Farm, Bell Farm.

When John Trethewey woke up in his comfortable English bed – he felt rested and happy. He raised himself up on his pillows and looked at his room by daylight. A square, low ceilinged room with dark beams – an open fireplace – the ash scattered from the wood fire he had enjoyed the night before – the lattice window was open and rose patterned curtains fluttered in the breeze – the sunlight streamed in, John sighed with contentment – he felt he had done the right thing to come to England. He stretched, yawned, ran his fingers through his hair. 'Now for Cornwall,' he said aloud to himself, as he sprang out of bed. Wrapping a towel round his waist and pulling off his nightshirt, he poured cold water into the wash basin on the wash stand, leant over and bathed his face, neck and torso – standing on the rush mat, he raised himself and splashed the cold water all about his person. He felt young, strong, fit, ready for anything the new life and new country might have to offer.

He dressed carefully and neatly. White cambric shirt, a soft black bow at the neck, Moleskin trousers and soft grey coat. He put a clean handkerchief in his breast pocket and standing in front of the mirror, carefully combed his damp dark hair.

Picking his wallet off the dressing table, he opened it, and looked inside for the card he had been given by George Trescawn, attorney. He slipped it back into his wallet, put it in the inside pocket of his jacket – crossed the room through a shaft of bright sunlight, an omen of good luck perhaps – opened the door and stepped out, feeling that he was stepping into an adventure, a new life was beginning.

Downstairs all was bustle. The tap room was full, everybody seemed to be talking at once, he caught the eye of a man across the room who put up his hand to him and signalled an empty chair at his table. John crossed over between the chairs with difficulty but arrived, laughing at the crush, and took his place at the table.

'Good morning,' he said. The other man sniffed a greeting.

'Yes, and it is a good morning,' he said 'the fog has gone and the sun's up and this is a mighty good breakfast, I recommend you, bacon and eggs, toast and strong coffee.'

'Sounds like a real English breakfast' John said, as he put his hand up to attract the attention of Mrs Jenkin. She came over as soon as she had unloaded her tray and was full of solicitude for his comfort. Had he had a comfortable night – slept well, not been awakened too early by the hustle and bustle on the harbour. John reassured her that he had been most comfortable and was well rested and refreshed and ready for anything, especially her bacon and eggs and whatever else she had to offer in the way of an English breakfast.

Mrs Jenkin disappeared through the door at the back into the kitchen and John turned to his companion, asked him his name and what his business was.

'Well, my name is Lewis Crago and I work in Borlase Bank,' he said, 'I live and work in Truro – that is down in Cornwall. Today I have come up to the Plymouth branch on business.'

'Ah!' said John, 'You might be able to help me, I have just come from Africa. My father was a Cornishman and a mine Captain, he went to Africa as a young man. Married out there. I am the only child. He died out there two years ago. Now my mother has died too. I buried her just over three weeks ago.

Going through my parents things I found old photographs of my father's home, a farm in Cornwall. My cousin farms there now so I have decided to buy a farm there too, to be near to my roots. The first thing to do is find a bank, place some money and securities in it – get some English money in my wallet and then I'm off to Cornwall to find my farm.

John settled his account at 'The Dolphin' and thanked Mrs Jenkin for her kind hospitality. She wished him well and hoped that he would soon find a suitable farm and establish himself in Cornwall. 'Anytime you have business in Plymouth you will always find a warm reception at 'The Dolphin',' she said, as she watched his tall figure stride away, accompanied by Lewis Crago – who had offered to show him the way to Borlase Bank and introduce him to the Manager, Thomas Hendry. She said to herself, as she turned to go indoors, 'He'm a proper gentleman, no mistake.'

Thomas Hendry received John with kindly courtesy, offered him a chair opposite his desk, listened to what he had to tell him. John told him about his parents death – the sale of his property in Africa and his journey to England. He told of his cousin James and his farm 'Rosewyn' at Cledra, inland from a place called Lancelot and how he intended looking for a farm that he could buy in that area. When he had finished, he opened his brief case and took out all the papers relating to his modest fortune, laying them on the desk in front of them. Mr Hendry asked if he wished to open an account at that moment. John said that he did, whereupon Mr Hendry summoned a clerk to bring all the necessary documents for him to sign. This done, he drew out a comfortable sum of money for his present needs, shook Thomas Hendry warmly by the hand and took his leave. He then went in search of George Trescawn the solicitor who had given him his card the night he had arrived at 'The Dolphin'. He took out his wallet and found the card – No.2 The Crescent, it said. He put the card back in his wallet, looked about him and accosted a passing stranger to ask him where The Crescent might be – the stranger was pleased to direct him, it was an easy matter as The Crescent could be seen behind some trees, no great distance from where they were standing. John thanked him and set off. It was a fine row of tall, well built stone houses, built in a half circle. No.2 was at the other end when he found it. He pulled a well polished brass bell beside the door and waited. After a few moments the door was opened by a fresh faced young man – John asked for Mr Trescawn – the young man smiled, stepped back and invited him to enter. He took off his broad brimmed felt hat, picked up his bags and followed the young man into a wide hall, well furnished with polished furniture and warm rugs – the young man motioned him to sit on a chair by the wall while he advised Mr Trescawn of his arrival. Mr Trescawn came out of his office and held out both hands to greet him.

'My dear fellow, come in at once, I am so glad to be of service to you. Tell me how you have faired since we met last night. Were you comfortable, did you sleep well.'

'Yes, many thanks – I was very well taken care of at 'The Dolphin' and this morning I have been to Borlase Bank to open an account and draw some money for my immediate needs.'

Once in the comfortable office, settled opposite each other, in high backed arm chairs, Mr Trescawn banged his knee with his hand and said, 'Well now young man, how can I be of service to you?' John put his hand in his pocket and took out his wallet and extracted the card with the words Bell Farm written on the back. He said as he handed it across,

'I heard some men talking last night as I ate my dinner, they mentioned this farm and said it would probably be for sale, do you know of it?'

'No, I don't know of it, but I can find out for you. I'll send my young man round to the agents. There are at least two in the town who handle that sort of property.' He rang a brass bell that stood on his desk, the fresh faced young man opened the door and looked enquiringly from one to the other. 'Albert, I want you to go round to the House Agent Pascoe, ask if they know of a property called Bell Farm on the market, or coming onto the market. They have two offices in Cornwall,' he turned to John, 'one in Truro and one in Lankard.'

When John had finished his business in Plymouth and settled his financial affairs and left them in the safe keeping of George Trescawn and Thomas Hendry, he made his way down to Cornwall. He was surprised to see how different Cornwall looked from Devon. Gone, the cosy hills and valleys, instead the trees were gnarled and windblown for the most part, all leaning away from the prevailing west wind. There were tall hedges of stone, covered with undergrowth. Banks of brilliant yellow gorse still in bloom, because the climate was so mild. There were other flowers enjoying a late summer. The roads were narrow and stony; the hills precipitous with tunnels of old trees meeting overhead, dripping their golden leaves which floated down and sailed away like little boats on the torrents of spring water that gushed down the gutters. The air under the trees and in the valleys was moist and smelt of gorse, heather and salt from the sea which surrounded this home county of his and was never far distant.

John received a tumultuous welcome from his cousin James and his wife Amy. 'Rosewyn' was built of granite, long and low, a porch at the front and half covered in a bright red creeper, giving it a warm, safe appearance. The ground floor had massive slate floors, shining like glass from years of elbow grease and polish. The furniture was dark and polished. The main living room had its original open hearth, with a heap of wood ash, kept piled with logs night and day. It pervaded the house with the lovely smell of wood smoke. John felt completely at home. This was what he wanted for himself, an old Cornish farmhouse surrounded by granite buildings full of fat cows and young calves, sheep in his fiends. Good strong horses to plough and till the land, dogs and cats, hens and ducks, a cockerel to crow in the morning and tell him it was dawn.

John had been with his cousin for two weeks, at the end of October, when he got up to find a letter waiting on the breakfast table. It was from George Trescawn. He wrote to say he had traced Bell Farm and yes it was for sale and there was to be an auction of farm stock and implements on November 6th. All particulars could be obtained from Thomas the Auctioneer in Lankard. Pascoe's the house agent was handling the sale of the farm.

That morning James put Polly his grey mare into the trap and he and John set off for Lankard and the agents. They put up the mare and trap at 'The Feathers' in the care of the old groom Jack. He was delighted to see James and Polly was an old friend. As the two cousins walked out of the yard, he looked after them, his hand on Polly's bridle. 'Who's the tall dark stranger you got with you today Polly?' Polly flicked her ears and rubbed her nose against his sleeve, to draw his attention to the fact that she wanted her nose bag of oats and a drink of water.

The two men caused quite a stir in Pascoe's office. James introduced his cousin and Mr Pascoe was excited and all of a flutter when John said that he had come to buy a farm and mentioned Bell Farm in particular.

'Why yes, yes!' said Mr Pascoe, Bell Farm only just on the market. There's been a death there, a sad business. The widow has only just decided to sell.' John smiled.

'I'm sorry about the death,' he said, 'but I am very interested in the farm. Can you give me all the particulars? I want a good substantial house and buildings, about hundred acres upwards.'

'Oh yes, it's all of that,' said Mr Pascoe. It's in good heart, Richard Kerris was a good farmer.' He drew two chairs together, they sat down and discussed details, as he told John how he should go about viewing and perhaps purchasing Bell Farm.

CHAPTER THREE
Joel Kerris

Joel Kerris' farm, 'Trevesa', was about four miles from the sea. Situated at the head of a small valley, it was sheltered, the worst of the storms went over its head. The windows rattled a bit and Joel sitting comfortably with his pipe in an old stick back chair in a corner of the kitchen by the polished Cornish slab – it's fire doors open, throwing out warmth and light, looked across at his wife Jinny, small, round and rosy, placidly knitting and thought about Sara – alone with Martha at Bell Farm. The wind would be strong there, coming straight in from the sea – lovely on a summer's day, but wild in winter. While Richard was alive, the house reverberated with the sound of his shouts and laughter – he was a big man and needed feeding. There was always a smell of baking – bread, buns, saffron cake, boiling ham or a roast. Sara was a good cook, but not little and round and comfortable like Jinny. She was tall, with dark hair and eyes, and a pale creamy skin – he could remember when they were married. People said 'she won't never make a farmer's wife, coming from the Manor like she do' – others said, 'look! She got spirit, she do ride a horse same as a man – don't 'ee go for to under estimate her' – they had been right.

Joel puffed at his pipe, his eyes half closed and remembered back over the years.

What a wedding that had been – a profusion of flowers in the Church from all the gardens in the village – the smell of wax from the lighted candles on the Altar and window ledges, out-did the smell of mould, and the flowers hid the damp patches on the walls. What an array of Sunday suits and shining boots – accompanied by billowing skirts, frills and flounces. Puffing his pipe and remembering he didn't think he had seen such an array of hats since. Big hats, small hats, ribbons of silk and velvet, flowers, feathers and some even had a bird or some fruit. New boots and shoes squeaked, as they came into Church and their wearers trod on tip toe hoping they wouldn't . Petticoats rustled and some showed a bit of lace at the hem. 'Lovely,' he thought, a pity the fashion had changed, with the turn of the century, 'too straight, with too much before and behind – didn't leave nothing for you to guess about now,' he mused to himself.

He stretched in his chair and shuffled a bit as he thought about how it had been on that wedding day. What a feast was prepared at Bell Farm Most wives in the village had had a hand in it. Aunt Mary, bless her, had supervised it all – (same as she did at the funeral he thought). Ned Semmens waited outside the Church with his wagonette and pair of matched grey horses – white ribbons plaited into their manes and a bow of white ribbon tied on to his whip – Bride and Groom came out of the Church in a snow storm of confetti and rose petals and laughing, almost ran to Ned for protection. Three little boys and three little girls running behind them, laughing and jostling each other and all piling into the wagonette – Ned flicked his whip, the white ribbons danced in the breeze, Bride and Groom and laughing children almost lost to sight in a sea of silks and tulle as Ned bore them to the farm for the feast.

Joel stretched and shuffled again. The stick-backed chair creaked under the strain. My what eating and drinking, cider cup – wine flowing and speech making, music and a song or two. Then a final speech to toast the Groom and the dark eyes of the Bride – Joel's thoughts stilled – he held the scene in his mind's eye – Richard took his Bride's face, so gently between his hands, turned her face up and kissed her on the lips – everyone fell silent – then he put his arm around her and drew her to the big oak stairs and slowly up and up, until lost to sight in the shadows above – downstairs, candle light and flowers everywhere – laugher broke out – everyone raised their glasses and talked at once – as the couple disappeared from sight. Joel's chin sank onto his chest as he re-lived the memory.

Jinny was getting on with her knitting – every now and then she rested her needles and looked across at Joel – 'I wonder what 'ee's thinking about,' she said to herself. Joel came to himself and felt her eyes upon him, sat up in his chair and wiped his face with his hand. 'What you thinking about,' she said, 'you been so quiet for some long time?'

'Oh 'ess Jinny, I been thinking back to Richard's wedding

to Sara – what a fine do that was, some lovely – music, singing, flowers, a feast – what dresses, ribbons and silks, billowing skirts and flounces – we ain't seen nothing like that since – now 'ess gone. Only one bairn to show for it and that be a girl.' Jinny stuck her chin out, 'Well she ain't no worse for that – you'll see she'll be beautiful like her mother – she'm tall now for her age and good strong limbs – everyone do love 'er, she's some good about the 'ouse and she love to be outdoors as much as in, you'll see Joel Kerris, Sara's Martha will make some man a beautiful bride yet!'

'You'll be right Jinny – you'm generally right – least ways I bin thinking of they two women over to Bell Farm by themselves. 'Tis October, gales are getting up, nights are dark – what they going to do? They can't run that great farm without a man – they men over there are getting old – they won't stand much longer without Richard!'

Jinny looked up and rested her knitting in her lap. ''Ees,' she said, 'you'm right, poor soul, I do feel some for 'er – she's some proud, but 'tis my belief she should sell that place – have a little place, all done up nice, she would have plenty then and no worry.' Joel puffed at his pipe and thought for a moment.

'I think you're right 'Mother', I'll go over there tomorrow and have a talk with her. It won't do to wait until the winter 'ave really set in.' He drew at his pipe, bit the stem and watched the smoke rising, thinking about what he would say.

As it was a lovely October day, a fresh wind, sunshine, a blue sky and clouds scudding high, Sara decided to do a big wash.

She collected up sheets, towels, pillow cases, table cloths, anything that needed to dry while the weather held fine and there was a good drying wind like today. She filled the clothes copper in the corner of the wash house, carrying up buckets of cold water from the pump in the yard, grated into it a bar of yellow soap on a suet grater, then carefully pushed in the linen with a well-washed wooden stick. This done, she put a match to the newspaper and sticks already laid in the grate below, the flames leapt, the sticks crackled, she piled in more wood and shut the door. This done, she left the wash to look after itself and went out into the yard. The sun shone, the clouds were bright with reflected light and the wind blew loose wisps of hair about her head and her apron billowed about her like a flag – for once she felt light hearted and care-free. She took the lid off the grain barrel and scattered handfuls of grain across the ground, calling to her hens – they came running from all directions, the wind, pushing them along and spreading their tails.

In the kitchen Martha, her arms covered in flour, a smudge of white flour on her check, was rolling out pastry for a rabbit pie – the dish beside her was full of rabbit joints, chopped bacon, chopped onions, herbs and hard boiled eggs – she hummed a little song to herself as she worked.

Sara had just finished her wash and pegged it out in the orchard between the trees – there were windfalls on the grass and the apples still on the trees were bright rosy red – she fixed the last peg, stooped and filled her basket with apples, stopping as she went back to the house to look at the golden stubble fields that stretched away to the blue horizon – sea gulls white against the blue, cried and screeched as they were blown about the sky like autumn leaves. Meanwhile Martha was just getting her pie from the oven, when she heard the sound of horses hooves and the scrunch of wheels on the gravel, outside the front garden gate. Putting the pie on its dish on the table, she squeezed round and peered out of the window. 'My 'tis cousin Joel!' she undid her flowery apron, wiped her face with it, flung it into a chair and ran to the back door – Sara stood among her hens, 'Mum!' she called, 'Cousin Joel is here! Just come in his trap with the cob Daisy – they're round the front!' Martha dashed in at the back door, ran to the front and arrived just as Joel banged on the big iron knocker.

She flung the door wide and there stood Joel, filling the doorway, laughing and holding out his arms to her. ''Ow are 'ee me beauty? 'Ow are 'ee then?' Martha flung herself into his arms and was hugged tight – he loosed her at last. 'Where is Sara then? ''Ow is she?' As he spoke Sara came hurrying, to be caught up in her turn in Joel's warm embrace. 'Sara, me dear, 'ow are 'ee then? 'Ow's the farm? They men doing alright for 'ee are they?' So laughing and talking all at once, they led him into the kitchen and pushed him into Richard's old arm chair, that still stood by the slab.

'Martha, fetch Joel a mug of cider,' turning to Joel she said, 'You'll have dinner won't you Joel?

'If it's that pie, smelling so good, I'll be glad of a bit of dinner,' he said. Martha returned with the mug of cider.

'There you are cousin Joel, I'll put a few more potatoes in the pan and we'll have the beans you sliced last evening Mother and I believe I'll put some apples to bake with brown sugar and a drop of cider.'

*

The meal over – Joel wiped his mouth with the big, white napkin Sara had provided. They had made a hearty meal and exchanged all their latest news. Joel pushed his chair back, it grated on the stone flagged floor, he gave a big long drawn out sigh. Belched – arf! Was silent for a moment then – 'I want to 'ave a talk with you Sara me dear, serious like, 'tis about the future.'

'What about the future Joel?'

'Well, 'tis all very well for you two women, running this here farm for a month or two, but you can't go on for ever by yourselves – you do need a man about the place. This 'ere is a big farm, there is a lot of business to see to besides the planting – you don't know the half, Sara me dear.' Sara knew what he was leading up to.

'You trying to tell me I must sell Bell Farm Joel Kerris – because no way am I going to do it.' She gave him a stony stare and pursed her lips tight.

'Don't take on Sara, you got to think about it – the farm is in good shape right now, the harvest is in, the fields are clean, the barn full of grain – been a good year too, showing a good crop you'd get a good price – October is a good month to sell.' Sara remained silent. Joel tried again. 'Look Sara, you got a nice little house over in Butterfield Meadow – if you was to keep that house and the meadow, you'd have a nice little place – you and Martha could manage that fine – you could have a few chickens, ducks and geese too, if you've a mind to – 'tis right on top of the garden there – you'd know how you'd love a garden and a bit of gardening? You could get Bert from up Tewan to come and do it up for 'ee. You could 'ave a bath and a new stove and 'ot water and you'd still 'ave a bit of Bell

Farm it wouldn't be all gone and you might get a good farmer to buy the farm and have good neighbours.' The talk went to and fro for most of the afternoon – for an against. 'Anyway you can think about it. I got to go now, Sara, the 'orse will be fretting and Jinney is anxious if it gets dark before I'm in.'

He got to his feet slowly, his legs were a bit stiff and straightened himself out – then he took Sara by the shoulders, kissed her on the cheek and looked seriously into her eyes, 'You think about what I've said Sara.' Then he turned to go, Martha went to see him off.

Outside he whistled loudly – a boy came out of the dusk leading his horse and trap – Joel felt in his pocket for a coin, gave it to the boy. He turned to Martha, 'Talk to her,' he said, 'She'll 'ave to come to it.' Giving her a big hug and a kiss, he mounted the step into the trap. 'Look after her mind!' He called out as he wrapped a rug about his knees. Taking up the reins and his whip he flicked it, shook the reins and clicked his tongue 'O'me me beauty,' he crooned to his horse, as they disappeared into the approaching night. Candle light from the carriage lamps on either side of the trap making warm light and shadows on the hedgerows as they went.

Martha stood looking after him until the trap and its warm light were out of sight. She went in and shut the back door, a big sigh escaped her as she joined Sara in the kitchen. Neither of them spoke, Martha took up the poker and rattled it under the fire – the ash dropped silently into the ash pan beneath – she took a big shovel of coal out of the bucket beside the hearth, took a ring off the top and shot in the coal. Dusty flames leapt up – she replaced the ring, put the poker and shovel back in their place and stood up looking at Sara sitting silent in her chair where Joel had left her.

'It's no good Mother,' she said, 'We shall 'ave to come to it – this 'ere is a great big place and it do feel empty without father – I don't like it really – I don't b'lieve you do neither – let us sell 'em and get a little place of our own like 'ee said.

Yes, it was October, the equinoxial gales had set it. Sara lay in her four poster bed, the curtains partially drawn about her and listened to the rain beating on the window – great gusts of wind rattling the window frames – enough to smash them. She thought of the great rolling waves that would be crashing on the rocks, maybe big enough to reach the grass land above them. There would be plenty of wood washed up – enough to keep them with fires in the parlour for many a month. 'I'll get Richard to go down with the men and fetch it up' she thought. Then – a cold clutch at her heart – no Richard, or ever would be again. 'He's gone – gone forever' – she whispered into the dark. Tears sprang to her eyes, she rolled over. They soaked into her pillow as she sobbed gently to herself remembering, it's forever – forever, she sobbed.

It was daylight when Sara woke. The wind still rattled the window and the rain beat against the glass so hard that it bubbled in at the bottom where the winter gales of many years had warped the frame. Sara watched a wet trickle of water trace a dark line down the faded wallpaper. She lay and thought about cousin Joel's visit and what he had said about selling the farm and doing up the cottage in Butterfield Meadow – Butterfield Meadow. The name pleased her. 'If I do it, if I'd move and do up that there cottage, I'll call it after the meadow,' she thought and the name and the idea pleased and warmed her. "Tis close to the cove, Martha will like that and like Joel said, we could 'ave a bath and water in the kitchen and perhaps a water closet inside – we wouldn't 'ave to go outside of a winter's day,' – she picture the rooms, low, latticed windows with window seats, a bit longer than square – curtains with flowers, not big heavy dark ones to keep out the draughts – a big kitchen at the back – 'knock all they little pantries and sculleries into one big room, a new kitchen range that won't smoke.' Sara smiled to herself at the happy thoughts passing thro' her mind. A great gust of wind rattled the window so hard the lattice flew open, the curtains flew up to the ceiling and the rain came in. Sara leapt out of bed and caught the window catch pulling it shut and secured it. 'Cousin Joel is right,' she said in a whisper to herself, 'We shall have to sell. I'll go in to town today and see Mr Pascoe the agent and tell 'um to sell.'

Sara drove her pony and trap into Lankard and put up at the stables behind the Feathers Hotel. Old Jack the stable man and groom smiled and touched his cap when he saw her – went forward and held the pony's head, while Sara throwing off the warm rug, clambered down. 'Give her a bit and a drink of water Jack,' she said, 'I shan't be more than an hour – I'm just going to have a word with Mr Pascoe.'

   She straightened her hat and settled her pelisse round her shoulders, gave Jack a nod, she picked up her skirts and set off into the town.

   Jack looked after her as she walked away, tall and straight. 'She'm a handsome woman,' he said to himself 'I'd wonder what she d'want with old Pascoe – maybe she'm going to sell.' He raised his cap and scratched his head, replaced it on his head and clucked to the pony – 'Come on Gyp he said you d'want a drink of water.' Gyp followed him across the yard. Jack took the pump handle and vigorously pumped it up and down. The water gushed out into a waiting bucket. Jack undid the traces on each side of her harness, lowered the trap shafts on to the ground. Taking hold of the bridle he led her into one of the hotel's waiting loose boxes patting and chatting to her – the while he undid buckles and straps and relieved her of her harness, which he flung over a partition – went to fetch a bundle of sweet hay and the bucket of water. Gyp whinnied gently to him by way of thanks and plunged her nose into the cold clean water – as he went out and bolted the door – she looked up lovingly – drops of water dripping from her nose – they were old friends – lowered her head and began to munch her hay.

Sara held up her skirt and picked her way along the pavements and over the cobbles until she came to a glass door with gold lettering on it 'Ernest Pascoe Auctioneer & Valuer' she read. She hesitated for a moment – then drawing herself up to her full height and straightening her shoulders, she made up her mind once and for all, lifted the latch and went in.

There was a pale looking man behind a desk, he looked up as she came in, pushed back his chair, stood up and came to meet her. 'Good morning', he said as he came round the desk to greet her.

'Good morning,' said Sara, 'Is Mr Pascoe in? If so I would like to talk to him on a matter of business.' The young man smiled.

'Yes,' he said, 'take a seat Mam while I fetch him,' and he pulled forward a chair. Sara sat down, after a few minutes the inner door opened and Mr Pascoe came out. A short stocky little man with round rosy face which broke into a welcoming smile when he saw who his visitor was. He came forward holding out his hand in welcome.

'Mrs Kerris! How do you do? What can I do for you?' turning to the young man he said, 'Wilfred pull up a chair for Mrs Kerris.' Wilfred pushed forward a black leather arm chair and helped Sara into it – then discreetly withdrew, quietly closing the door.

Sara began at once, 'Mr Pascoe,' she said, 'I'm going to sell – yes – I'M going to sell Bell Farm.' Mr Pascoe made a depreciating gesture, Sara continued, 'I've thought about it a lot, there is no other way. The men I've got are old, without my husband they won't be able to manage. I want you to find me a good farmer, who'll keep the farm in good heart.

'What are you thinking of doing?' he asked. 'Where do you and your daughter plan to live?'

'Well,' Sara said, 'we have decided to keep the field on the edge of the land that has a quite large cottage on it – we plan to do some alterations, like putting in a bath – bringing the water into the house – having a kitchen range with a boiler – having hot water and maybe a water closet in the house.'

Mr Pascoe nodded and smiled his approval – 'Well I think you will be very wise' he said, 'Bell Farm is a big rambling old house – it needs a f family in it – what is the field called where the cottage stands?' He opened a drawer and took out a map of the area around the farm and spread it out on his desk. 'What is the cottage called?' he asked.

'The field is called Butterfield Meadow and I plan to call the cottage by that name,' she said and smiled a warm smile. Mr Pascoe could see that she was pleased with the thought and the sound of Butterfield Meadow. He liked it himself, it sounded comfortable and homey.

'Right! Mrs Kerris – you leave the matter in my hands. 'I'll see if I can find the right buyer for you, it shouldn't be difficult – a lovely farm – lovely farm,' he repeated to himself as he made a few notes. 'If this is what you want – I'll get on with it right away.' He looked up and smiled with a twinkle in his eyes, 'Meanwhile I think you will be quite safe to get on with your alterations to Butterfield Meadow.

CHAPTER FOUR
Butterfield Meadow

Once Sara had made up her mind to sell the farm, she felt a lot happier. She had known all along that that was what she had to do, but taking the final step and putting it in the hands of the agent was a big step to take and seemed so final. However, once she had seen Mr Pascoe, she left his office feeling as though a weight had been lifted from her shoulders. 'I will get it all done at once,' she thought and made her way through the town to the auctioneer's office to put in motion the sale of the farm stock, and implements. Dan Wilkes was in his office and kept her waiting only a few moments while he dealt with another client. He listened to all she had to say with kindly concern, but he did not question her wisdom in deciding to sell and determined to do his best for her. Sara spent an hour discussing the details with him – they fixed the date of the sale for November 6th.

After leaving the auctioneer, she went to the stables and

collected Gyp and the trap. Gyp knew her step and whinnied as she approached – Sara was emotionally moved when she heard him – she felt as though a friend had laid a hand on her shoulder, it was a strange experience, it gave her a feeling of security, even though her whole life lay broken about her.

Jack led Gyp out of the stable and harnessed him to the trap – Sara thanked him and gave him a florin – he took her elbow and helped her to climb up – putting the reins into her hands, he smiled and touched his cap – 'Good day Mam,' he said as she shook the reins and Gyp walked forward and out of the cobbled yard.

Once free of the town, they trotted along happily, it was a warm October day – the sun cast a golden light over the hedgerows and little coveys of young sparrows darted along in front of them – flying swiftly from one clump of brambles to another, chirping to each other as they went.

Sara decided to drive past Jim Thomas' house. He was the builder, she thought best fitted to repair and improve her cottage in Butterfield Meadow. She stopped the trap in the lane outside the gate, got down and hitched the reins over the iron railings – banged the black painted iron knocker on the door and waited. Jim came to the door in his working trousers – his braces hitched over a striped flannel shirt – no collar and a brass stud at the neck. He was swallowing a mouthful of dinner.

''Ullo! Mrs Kerris,' he exclaimed in surprise – Sara smiled.

'Hullo Jim – I want you to do something for me,' he grinned.

'What would that be then, Mrs Kerris?'

'I'm going to sell Bell Farm and move to the cottage in

Butterfield Meadow, will you do it up for me?' she smiled at him. He looked very surprised and sucked his teeth.

'Oh 'ess! Mrs Kerris. Sure I will – do 'ee want it done right away like? I best come over and see you about it,' he scratched his head. 'I got a job to finish this afternoon, I'll come over in the morning – see what you d'want – 'ow will that suit you?'

'That will be nice Jim, we will go over to the cottage and decide what it is best to do.'

Jim was true to his word. He arrived at about nine o'clock. It was a lovely October day, bright sunshine with a golden Autumn tinge to it, fluffy white clouds sailing high. Sara was in the yard when he drove in. He jumped down from his trap and hitched the reins to an iron ring by the stable door and walked over to her.

'Mornin! Mrs Kerris.'

'Good morning Jim – what a lovely morning!'

'Ess – 'ee is too – shall I drive 'ee over to Butterfields then?'

'Why yes, if you've a mind too – that would save me putting up Gyp.'

'Well there ain't no call for two traps is there?'

'Well no Jim, just wait here a minute, while I take off my apron and put on a jacket.'

They drove the short distance to the cottage, chatting all the way. Sara told Jim of her ideas to build up the lean-to at the back, making a large kitchen below right across the house and upstairs a bathroom with a WC and another bedroom. 'Do you think we could do all that Jim?'

Jim slowed the pony to a walk and was thoughtful – 'Well,' he said, 'the bathroom upstairs do depend on what head of water e've got, but maybe we can catch'n off of the roof – 'spect I'll manage 'em somehow – don't go for to worry. The rest I think will be easy.'

They came to the gate – Jim jumped down – opened it and led the pony through.

Sara was taken by surprise. The cottage looked bigger than she remembered it. Grey Cornish stones, the top half reinforced by old rag slates. The small square panes of the windows blinking in the sunlight.

Sara got down from the trap, took a big heavy key from her pocket, pushed open the gate into the front garden. She saw overgrown dead grass plots surrounded by flower borders here and there a splash of yellow from the bravely golden rod – defying the neglect. Sara clicked her tongue and tossed her head, went on and unlocked the front door – it squeaked as she pushed it open. The hinges wanted oiling. The floor boards were bare and littered with Autumn leaves blown under the door – a spider scuttled quickly out of sight surprised by the bright sunshine that flooded the little passage – when the door was opened. Sara went cautiously forwards – feeling as if she were about to disturb someone. Jim took his cap off and held it before his chest as he stood behind her – both stood quite still and were silent for a moment. The spirits of people who had dwelt there many years before holding them in a spell. There came a gust of Autumn wind. The door banged shut behind them, they laughed and their voices echoed in the empty house. Sara pushed open a door and looked into a room that had once been the parlour – panelled cupboards either side of an open fireplace – a small heap of dead ash on the hearth and lumps of soot that had fallen down the chimney – there were dry sticks and a few feathers – Jim looked up the chimney, 'a bird's nest in un' I shouldn't wonder' he said. There was a window seat with spider's webs and cracked paint. But even so, Sara could see in her mind, bright white paint – chintz curtains, books and pieces of bright china – a crackling fire of sticks and logs on the hearth – yes, she could make a home here. They went out into the lean-to at the back – it had dark brown paint, a small cracked window, a rusty old Cornish slab – the smell of mould, damp and dirt.

'This is where we'll make the kitchen,' she said, 'a big room right across – knock all these little dark places into one – put in a good window – a new stove – a sink with a pump to it. This could be a lovely room, warm and sheltered. We could make a porch at the back for boots.' Jim followed her about, making notes in his notebook and nodding his head. As they went from room to room, Sara told him her ideas.

Jim said he thought it was all possible, he would start first thing on Monday morning.

It was mid-day by the time they had finished the whole cottage and the small outbuildings. They must make a wash-house with a copper to boil the clothes. A place for tools and a wheelbarrow, to lay out the apples and onions for the winter.

As Sara stood with Jim outside the front door, discussing the minor details, she turned and looked towards the sea. The field stretched away before her, in the distance, the blue, blue sea – white horses galloping, flinging mountains of white spray against the rocks. Gulls were circling overhead screeching at the Autumn wind. Sara had a strange feeling of being already at home, such was the peace and tranquillity.

Back at the farm, Martha had dinner ready. The kitchen table laid, there was boiled fowl, parsley sauce and lemon, boiled potatoes and broccoli, followed by baked apples and clotted cream. Jim thanked them for the meal, afterwards making copious notes and diagrams.

During the days that followed, the farm men dragged out all the farm machinery and implements, while Sara and Martha made several trips to the cottage. They took a picnic and some gardening tools and set about cleaning the ragged borders. The sun shone, the clouds sailed high, the gulls wheeled and cried and in the distance they heard the sound of the sea. They were dirty and windblown and happy. Sara felt grateful to cousin Joel. She knew in her heart that she had done the right thing and was happy.

CHAPTER FIVE
The Sale

The men at Bell Farm worked hard and diligently preparing for the sale of the stock and implements that was to take place on November 6th. They turned out every nook and cranny – unearthing long forgotten rusty tools, laying them out in rows in the field, alongside the good and more modern implements. There were ploughs, scufflers, harrows, chain harrows, sets of harness – their brasses polished like new. Shovels, forks, rakes, spades, heavals, pikes, ropes, wagons, carts. Nothing was spared.

The day before the sale Sara and Martha toured the sad and silent rows – testimony to Richard's hard work and diligence. Sara put her hand on the wooden handle of a plough, so smooth and shiny from the grasp of his strong hands. She let her mind wander a little (though she had promised herself that she wouldn't, that she would be entirely practical). She saw him again – ploughing a long furrow, sea mist lightly veiling him. A flurry of white gulls about his head, waiting for the worms and grubs the plough would turn up, circling, diving, screeching, fighting. In the distance, she heard again the call of the sea as it pounded the ageless rocks. A big sigh escaped her – she patted the handle of the plough twice, absentmindedly, as she remembered those happy days 'gone, all gone – forever,' she whispered. She recalled herself, shrugged, straightened her shoulders and passed on down the lonely rows. Martha joined her. Interested, excited, looking to the future, 'I wonder who've bought the farm? I wonder if he've got a wife and family – he might have a daughter, same age as me. That would be nice company wouldn't it? We could go to Cove together,' so she chattered on. They came to the end of the last row, turned and retraced their step. They were now installed in Butterfield Meadow and had to walk the short distance from the farm to the cottage. Martha suddenly darted off in the direction of the stables.

'Where you going?' Sara called after her.

'Wait a minute for me,' Martha called back. 'I'm going to the stables to say goodbye to Lady and Prince - I won't be more than a minute or two.' She hitched up her skirt, ran the short distance to the field gate and into the stable yard. It was late afternoon, the sun low in the sky – a shaft of golden light shone fitfully through the dusty, cobwebbed window, highlighting Prince's dapple coat.

They heard her coming and whinnied to her. She slid into Lady's loose box – Lady backed away from the door, put her head down, breathed heavily and nuzzled her with her nose. Martha put her arms around her neck and buried her face in her silky mane. Tears sprang to her eyes, her throat ached, she found she couldn't speak. Prince whinnied from the adjoining box. Martha kissed Lady's nose and gave a last hug – turned and went to Prince. He stood, tall and proud looking over his door at her – she drew back the bolt and opened the door. He stood back as she entered. She put her hand up and stroked his velvet nose 'Oh Prince! – Prince!' she whispered, 'You're going to have to leave us – we got to go and you got to go. Be a good boy mind – ef you'm a good boy you'll be happy, no one won't hurt you – Oh Prince! Prince!' She sobbed and clung to his neck. He tossed his head up and down and nuzzled her with his soft white nose. Sara called, the light was fading, the shaft of sunlight had disappeared. She was alone with the cobwebs, the two great horses and her memories. Sara called again.

'Martha! Martha! Where'm you to? 'Tis getting late, we best be going.'

Martha gave a last pat, slid out of the stable and bolted the door, blew a kiss to Lady and ran across the yard to the field gate calling, 'Coming Mother – coming!'

They walked silently across the dusky field towards Butterfield Meadow. The sun had set, leaving a red glow on the skyline beyond the sea. Neither spoke. Their hearts were too full for words.

Reaching the meadow, leaving the farm behind, hearing the sea rising and falling with gentle waves upon the rocks, they felt comforted. It was almost dark when they reached the cottage and went in by the back door took off their boots in the new porch – opened the door into the lovely kitchen that Jim Thomas had made them. The warmth of their new kitchen range (the slab as they called it) reached out to welcome them. They were home. The fire had sunk low, Martha opened the fire doors, took the poker from the fender and riddled – the cinders were still hot and red, she put on a few shovels of small coal, flames leapt up filling the kitchen with flickering light. Sara drew the red flowered curtains, lifted the glass globe of a pink china lamp that she had left ready on the scrubbed pine table. She struck a match, turned up the wick, lit it, replacing the globe. The kitchen was filled with soft light, revealing the blue dinner service on the pine dresser, that Jim had built for them and the row of shining copper saucepans arranged on top. There was a new sink, and a pump indoors, as Sarah had planned. Martha took an iron kettle, filled it at the pump and put it on to boil. Sara had gone upstairs to tidy her hair, take off her heavy shawl and put her slippers on. Everything smelt clean and fresh, the smell of new paint lingered. The entrance passage inside the front door had a red carpet which went all the way upstairs onto the small landing – it was warm to her stocking feet.

There were three candles on an oak table on the landing. Sara lit two and took one into her bedroom – she had chosen a pale pink paper with apple blossom on it for her room – the curtains were made of a deep rose-coloured cambric – the carpet was also a deep rose colour with a border of green trellis. The whole effect was one of rest and peace. She sighed as she looked at herself in the mirror and smoothed her hair – gone was the drawn look of deep mourning. 'Yes' she said to herself, 'Joel was right. This is much better for Martha and me – it really feels like home.' A large cupboard big enough to walk into opened off her room – inside a mahogany wash stand with a china jug and basin covered with more roses and green leaves. Sara poured a little water into the basin and washed her hands, as she dried them on a linen towel she looked about her with pleasure – everything was so clean and fresh and dainty. Nothing to remind her of the hard work of a farmer's wife. She sighed, threw down the towel, took a light shawl off a hook and wrapped it round her shoulders, blew out the bedroom candle and put it back on the table on the landing – leaving the other alight for Martha. She met Martha at the bottom of the stairs where she had lit a lamp on a table in the hall. The light shone on her, highlighting the golden glint of her hair – Sara looked at her and thought her beautiful – creamy skin – the rosy bloom of a peach on her cheeks – bright eyes – she laughed up at Sara as she waited at the foot of the stairs.

'Mum you look beautiful – perhaps it's the lamplight – but you d'look real beautiful.' They passed each other – Martha ran up the stairs light foot to wash and tidy herself. Sara went into the kitchen – got out the cups and saucers – arranged them on a tray. The kettle was boiling – she warmed the tea pot and made the tea, arranged some rock buns on a plate and found a jar of new bramble jelly and cut a few slices of bread and butter. Martha returned, they sat down together in the warm kitchen – the fire doors open, the red coals glowed and the pink china lamp threw a golden glow over all.

The move from the farm had been sad. They had to leave so many things behind – it had been very difficult to choose what they would take – in the end it had been the things that would best fit into the cottage. Butterfield Meadow dictated its own terms – showed them the way – dispelled their misgivings and comforted their sorrows. Now it was done – they had three pretty bedrooms, one each and one for a visitor. A large parlour, with cream paper patterned with peach coloured roses and green leaves. A soft green carpet and plain green plush curtains for winter – they planned to have plain green cambric in the summer. Then there was the new kitchen – Sara loved it. The scrubbed pine table from the scullery at the farm. (The kitchen table had been too big) and a pine dresser built by Jim. The floor was of big slate slabs and there was a new rag rug in front of the slab. They sat, silent, for a while. Martha was hungry and eagerly ate bramble jelly on her bread and butter – drank a whole cup of tea, poured out another and took a large bit out of a rock bun. Sara sat quiet, a cup of tea in her hand – her mind going back and then forward, dwelling first on her memories, happy as well as sad – then on her hopes for the future. Neither of them had met the man who had bought the farm. The sale had been conducted privately by Pascoe the house agent, she believes the new owner came from away – she hoped he had a nice wife and family – a friend for her and for Martha – 'No matter, we shall meet him tomorrow I expect,' she thought.

Martha looked at her, 'Come on Mother – eat up your tea, the jelly is some lovely and I believe I've made these rock cakes as good as you'. They ate and drank in silence for a bit – they would be glad when the sale was over and all responsibility for the farm lifted from their shoulders.

The morning of November 6th broke, frosty and clear – the sun rose up over the hill behind the cottage with shafts of Autumn gold, the sky was blue. The distant sea a restless calm, scattered with white horses. Sara and Martha woke

early with the feeling of a day full of urgency. They dressed tidily – long tweedy woollen skirts. Sara wore a white blouse and pinned a Cameo brooch that Richard had given her one Christmas, at her throat. Martha wore a blue skirt with a softer blue blouse. The colour complemented her blue eyes and soft brown hair, bleached in places to a fine gold by the sun. They made hot porridge, with treacle and cream, followed by home cooked ham and bread and butter and a pot of tea, for their breakfast. When they had finished, Martha washed up while Sara made a packet of ham sandwiches for their picnic. They meant to stay at the sale all day to see who was there and who bought what.

When they arrived at the farm the men were there to greet them. George Pearce the horseman was in the stable grooming Lady and Prince who had their noses tucked happily in to their oats in their mangers. Martha ran to the stable, George looked over his shoulder and saw her silhouetted by the sunlight in the open doorway. 'Morning Miss – alright are 'ee?'

''Es, I s'pose – I got to 'aven't I? Oh Lady!' She went to Lady's head and kissed and smoothed her silk coat – then darted round to Prince to give a last kiss and pat.

'Don't take on Miss – they're going to be alright – they'll find a good home and maybe they'll stay here – the new farmer may want 'em, he got to 'ave 'orses 'aven't 'ee?'

''Es George, you're right, I mustn't worry for 'em.' She left the stables and went out into the sunshine. The sun was warm and the yard was full of people – men, women and children running all over the place, chasing each other round the carts and wagons, climbing up and pretending to be horses or driving them. She went to the field gate – there were people everywhere – examining the tools, trying them for strength, testing the blades of scythes and bill hooks – turning buckets upside down to see if there were any holes. Dan Wilkes the auctioneer arrived with his small band of helpers carrying papers and ledgers, pens and pencils, anything else he might need to conduct his business. He was followed by a man carrying two wooden chairs and another carrying a large wooden box. They set these up on a wagon inside the field and farmers and their wives from far and near as well as working men and village folk, began to gather in a seething mass. Pushing, shoving and all talking at once – all anxious to be in the forefront to see and be seen.

Sara and Martha wandered off – Martha to the stables to talk to Lady and Prince, Sara to her hens in the orchard – they were scratching and pecking away under the apple trees, eating wind fallen apples, finding fat grubs inside. Sara lifted the lid of a corn bin by the gate and through a handful of grain to them – they turned and ran to her. She made a lovely picture – standing in the dapple shade beneath the apple trees. The long grass brushing her skirt – white hens feeding all around her. She nearly jumped out of her skin when a tall dark stranger emerged from the shadows and dropped his hat to her.

'Good day Mam – I hope I didn't frighten you none?' Sara had jumped and put her hand on her bosom, an involuntary movement, she tried to dispel any idea he might have of her shock, by putting her hand up and smoothing her hair which was blown wispy by the wind.

'Oh no,' she said, 'I'm just taking my leave of the hens. I've been here twenty years, it is sad to have to part with ones home, hens, horses, cows, calves, pigs and the like, when you have helped to rear them. They are like my children. I only hope the new owner will buy some of them – he's bound t'want horses, he can't do without them – they're beautiful too – strong and good workers.'

'How many have you got?'

'Three, Lady and Prince, on the farm and little Gyp the pony for the trap.'

'I see, I suppose they're in the stables – I should like to go and see them – which way do I go?'

Sara indicated the stable yard – he replaced his hat.

'Good day to you Mam – it's been nice making your acquaintance,' he bowed to her and strode off in the direction of the stables.

Martha had left Prince and Lady and was now sitting on a pile of straw in Gyp's stable – they were both eating juicy red windfalls. Martha was chatting happily – 'You're not going anywhere my love – darling Gyp – we need you. We can't do nothing with they big horses, they're for farm work, but we need you for the trap, don't you worry nobody ain't going to take you away. But I am some sad for Lady and Prince – I don't know where they'm going – they won't know where they'm to either.' A shadow fell across the floor, the door opened and a tall stranger walked in – Martha went to stand up but she lost her balance in the straw and fell backwards, loosing her half eaten apple which rolled into the drain. He reached out and offered his hand.

'Here let me help you – I'm so sorry, did I frighten you? I met the lady from the farm in the orchard and she told me there were horses in here. I love horses, I've spent many hours in the saddle – I came in to see them. Perhaps you will tell me their names.' He had caught her hand and pulled her to her feet – she stood brushing the straw from her skirt, there were wisps of it in her hair – he put out his hand to help her – she backed away from him, blushing furiously. He picked up a piece of straw and put it in the corner of his mouth, tilted his head to one side and smiled at her.

'I'm sorry, I surprised you – I should have knocked, shouldn't I?' She threw back her head and laughed – her blue eyes flashing, untidy gold flecked hair, and a row of pearly teeth.

'No 'tis alright – I didn't know anyone was about – thought they were all in the field.' She went to the door of Gyp's stall and rubbed his nose wet with apple juice. 'This here is Gyp, I just told him he needn't fear he's going home with us to Butterfield Meadow.'

'Why, where is that – is it near here?' he asked. She went off into another peal of laughter.

'Don't you know where Butterfield Meadow is?' Then she sobered and looked hard at him. 'You'm new about here aren't you? Where do you come from then Lunon or somewhere?'

'No! Actually I come from Africa!'

'Africa?'

'Yes, Africa, have you heard of it?'

'Well yes,' she wrinkled her brow – well I spose I have but I don't know where it is, where is it?'

'It's rather difficult to explain – if you don't know – but its across the sea – I've only been in England three weeks. You see my Mother and Father are both dead.'

'Oh dear! You'm an orphan! I am some sorry, got any brothers or sisters 'ave you?'

'No.'

'What's your name then?'

'John'.

'John what?'

'John Trethewey.'

'Why that's a Cornish name! We got a neighbour called Trethewey – James Trethewey 'ee is – up to 'Rosewayn', that's a farm a few miles back.'

'I see.'

'Shall we go and see Lady and Prince?' she said leading the way out of the small stable. Coming to the big stable as she called it, he went before her and drew the bolt, opened the door and stood back for her to go first. Lady and Prince whinnied – she went first to lady and then to Prince – kissed their soft noses. 'My love – who's my love then,' she crooned. She turned to look at him over her shoulder. 'I love 'em' she said and there was a sob in her voice and her blue eyes became moist and misty. He went forward and patted them.

'Hullo Lady and Prince,' he said, 'Are you good workers?'

'A'course they are – they wouldn't be my father's horses unless they were good – my father was the best farmer for miles around, 'ain't no man to touch him – you walk around this farm some time and you'll see, but if you'm from a city, you wouldn't know would you?'

'No' he said. She couldn't make him out – he wasn't like a stranger – talking to her like he was a friend – very gentle like, but big and strong. 'I'm going to walk round and see how the sale is going – I haven't been to a sale before – I expect you want to stay with the horses, are they to be sold?' 'Yes – I suppose' – she turned from him and laid her cheek against Prince's nose, he rubbed his head up and down, he knew, but didn't understand her sadness.

Dan Wilkes shouted himself hoarse – his hammer rose and fell – his clerk scribbled in his ledger – the people, pulled an ear, flicked a thumb, waved a hat, nodded their heads and waved their hands – they all had various ways of clinching a bargain. The sale progressed, almost every little thing had somebody in need of it – the hammer fell for the last time. The crowd dispersed and peopled jostled each other as they hurried to collect their purchases and make a quick getaway.

Dan Wilkes got stiffly to his feet and stretched – took off his hat and scratched his head and put it on again. His clerk made the last entry in his ledger while his junior partner stowed cash and cheques safely away as fast as it was handed in.

The field was a hive of activity. Ponies and traps, horses with carts or wagons were loaded up, as if by magic, tools, implements and brick-a-brac were cleared from the trampled grass.

As the sun drew towards the west the whole sky was suffused with a rosy glow.

George Pearce put Gyp to the trap and led her out into the yard. Sara and Martha were waiting, he helped them mount, tucking a rug about their knees. Sara took the reins – George opened the gate into the lane – now cleared of buyers, clicked her tongue – slapped Gyp's rump 'get up their my beauty' he said, Gyp jumped forward at his touch and started the short distance to the cottage, little did she know that there was a newly furbished stable waiting for her – a manger of oats, a brand new hay net and water bucket.

Clip, clop! Clip, clop! Clip, clop! the sound of Gyp's hooves, and the rustling leaves, as the birds settled themselves for the night, comforted Sara and Martha as Gyp carried them homewards – 'Yes' Sarah thought 'homewards' to Butterfield Meadow – the shadowy hedgerows slipped by in the dusky evening light. It was November, the evenings were drawing in. They could see well enough by the fading daylight and had not bothered to light the lamps on the trap finding the twilight comforting after the hustle and bustle of the day.

Janie Pearce, George's grand-daughter had been at the cottage all day. Looking after Shep, tidying up after their early departure. She had lovingly prepared the stable for Gyp, lit a lantern and hung it on a nail. Made a deep bed of new season's yellow straw, filled a bucket with water, stuffed the new hay net, filled with happiness, as she stood in the deep glow from the lantern's light by the stable door and surveyed the comfortable scene. She pictured to herself Gyp's delight when he arrived and saw the comfort awaiting him at his new home, as tho' it were for herself. She took a broom and swept loose straw to make a tidy edge at the entrance and put it back against the wall. Leaving the lantern hanging on the nail, by its soft light she ran back across the yard to the cottage. It was now almost quite dark in the warm kitchen. She took a paper spill from a jar on the mantelpiece and lit it at the fire, carried its little flame to the oil lamp on the table, lifted the globe, turned up the wick and lit it. In a drawer in the dresser she found a red table cloth and spread it on the kitchen table. She fetched the cups and saucers with faded roses on them, put the fat old tea pot on the corner of the slab to warm while the kettle boiled. She cut a plate of bread and butter, filled a glass dish with new Victoria plum jam. My! It tasted good as she licked her sticky fingers. All was as ready as she could make it to welcome them home.

Arriving at the gate of the back yard, Martha jumped down and held it open while Sara drove Gyp through. A stream of light shone from the open stable door and another streak of light shone from the kitchen window. The yard was filled with a warm welcome. Sara's heart gave a flutter and a leap of joy. They had left the sadness, the dark emptiness of the farm behind. Martha took Gyp out of the trap undoing the traces and dropping the shafts – she led him into his new stable. He hesitated at the door, dazzled by the light from the lantern, although Martha thought him dazzled by the sight of his loose box, golden straw knee high and bulging hay net. She took off his harness, slipped the collar from his shoulders and the bridle from his head and hung them on a wooden peg on the wall. Then she patted his rump, he moved forward, his feet rustling thro' the thick straw. He buried his nose in his water bucket and Martha heard him swallowing long draughts of water. When he had slaked his thirst he lifted his dripping nose from the bucket and made his way to the manger, put his nose in, found his oats and began to munch – crunch, crunch, crunch, Martha listened with delight to his happy comfort for a second or two, then she shut his door softly, slipped the bolt in place, blew out the lantern and was gone away across the yard to the lighted kitchen window. She wiped her boots on the mat, lifted the latch of the back door and was home.

Sara, Martha and Janie ate bread and butter by the light of the pink oil lamp and drank hot tea from the rosy cups. Martha told Janie all about the sale. 'My! There was some people there, they've took all the stuff – loaded up carts and wagons, they did – bought up everything whether it was any good or not. They all 'ad to 'ave something.

There was a tall stranger there – I dunno what he was doing – he came into the stable – I was eating an apple with Lady and Prince – gave me a fright. I fell on my back in the straw and 'ee standing there laughing at me – I tell you I was some embarrassed!' She laughed at the memory and her eyes danced in the lamp light. 'Give me his hand he did – pulled me up and we had a good laugh.'

'What was 'ee called?'

'I dunno.'

'Didn't you ask 'im?'

'No – I never thought about it', Sara said thoughtfully, cradling her cup with both hands. 'He came into the orchard – I was with the hens, I gave them a handful of corn to make them come running, just once more – looked up, there he was. Didn't hear him coming, he stood inside the gate and took off his hat to me.'

'What was 'ee like?'

'I dunno Janie – very polite, tall, dark hair – sort of kind – like he was sorry to be there.' Sara was thoughtful, Martha was excited.

'Maybe he has bought the farm – maybe he was having a look around – didn't want to be known just yet, not before the sale anyway.'

Janie helped Martha clear the table and wash the tea things

in the sink – they laughed and chattered like two children, exchanging all sorts of romantic notions about the tall dark stranger.

The winter was past, the birds nesting and primroses were peeping from the hedgerows. Spring was here at last. Sara straightened her back and stood resting a moment, one hand on the handle of her fork – she had been digging a border round the little garden in front of her cottage. Richard had been dead nearly a year now and life had to go on. She had sold the farm to John Trethewey, a mining engineer just home from Africa, with a cousin farming inland from the coast.

She had brought a basketful of seedlings from the farm, forget-me-nots, marigolds, snapdragons, a lavender and rosemary bush. They were now planted in her newly dug border. She stood and imagined them in bloom – blue and gold. She would fill pots with them in the summer – how they would brighten up her little room. She constantly thought of it as her little room – but really it was quite a big room – the area of the whole cottage. Jim Thomas had done wonders, building another storey on top of the large lean-to at the back – making a nice square kitchen with the windows east and west. He had installed a new Cornish slab, Sara's pride and joy, and a small hand pump to get cold water from the tank without going outside into the yard.

There were rosy curtains at the windows, made out of bedroom curtains from the farm. A shiny polished slate floor, a rag rug in front of the slab. Sara went round to the back through a small gate at the side of the house, which opened onto a flagged path that let to the yard. Here she took off her boots in the porch and went into the kitchen. The cosy warmth reached out to greet her – the fire doors were open, the coals burned red and glowing. She took the kettle to the stone sink and poured some hot water into a bowl to wash her hands, filled the kettle with fresh water from the pump and put it on to boil. Drying her hands slowly on a small towel, she gazed out of the west window. It was mid April, the evenings were lighter, the sun drawing towards the west coast, a golden glow over the fields. The birds were busy flying to and fro with worms and grubs for their nestlings. Across the meadow she could see the blue and gold haze of bluebells, wild daffodils and patches of primroses all over the hedge. She sank into a large stick back arm chair beside the warm slab and closed her eyes, while the kettle boiled.

Martha was striding across Butterfield Meadow, the faithful Shep like a shadow at her heels, her apron full of kindling wood, gathered in the hedgerows – a posy of primroses clasped in her hand, hair blowing in the wind, full of the joys of spring. The move from the farm was completed, the physical and emotional strain lifted. She felt free as the air and the birds around her – a new life was beginning.

The back door was unlatched – she backed in with her bundle of wood – rosy and windblown – Sara awoke with a start – looking at her daughter, she thought she had never seen her look so lovely – the carefree life suited her. The sadness behind her, the move over. The kettle was spitting and hissing on the stove. She got to her feet and fetched the tea pot, measured out the tea and poured the boiling water over it. Martha let go her apron, dropping the bundle of sticks into the fender – she laughed and scraped the hair from her face. 'That'll keep us going for some while Moma.'

'Where've you been Martha to gather all that?'

'Oh, I been down to the cove with Shep. The spring tide have brought a brave lot o' wood in. I'll fetch some o' that another time – this 'ere, I got round the hedge as I came back. I'll tell you what Moma, its some handsome to be able to go down to beach so easy like and he do love it, don't 'ee Shep.' Shep wagged his tail and looked up at her, lips drawn back showing all his teeth in a doggie smile. Martha smiled back at him as she washed her hands at the sink. Meanwhile Sara put a check cloth on the end of the kitchen table, set down the tea tray, a plate of fresh baked Heavy cake. She sat herself at the end of the table and Martha drew up a chair and joined her. They sipped the hot tea and ate the crunchy cake, with nutmeg and sultanas in it, sugar sprinkled over the top. Sara ate slowly, with a feeling of peace – like a ship that has safely reached harbour after a storm. She enjoyed watching Martha eating two pieces of cake in quick succession – sipping her tea, laughing as she told of the cove below the meadow and the big pools where she would bathe when the summer came. She told of the cave that she had found at the far end, big enough to walk upright in – she had gone far enough inside to lose the daylight at the entrance.

'One day I'll go right in till I can't go no further, and see where it do lead.'

'Don't 'ee go for to do anything dangerous – you don't know where it d'lead to – the rock might fall and then you'd be shut in.'

'Oh 'tis quite safe Moma – I got Shep with me, he'd bark

loud enough! But 'tis some exciting.' They ate in silence for a while – Sara felt happier and more at peace than she had felt at all since Richard's death – the move to Butterfield Meadow had been a wise decision though it had taken her some time to make up her mind to do it. She thought back to cousin Joel's visit on a cold October day.

She hadn't wanted to listen to him, but he had been very persuasive, Martha had added her spoke too – she liked the idea, the thought of being so close to the sea, the sound of the waves lapping gently in fine weather – whispering to the rocks, rocking the gulls to sleep, then thundering in on stormy days, great rollers dashing over the rocks, covering the bottom of the field with spray like a sea mist. Martha was glad cousin Joel had persuaded Moma to move. They decided to call the little house 'Butterfield Meadow after the name of the field. Martha liked to imagine yellow and white cows grazing in the lush grass and giving lots of lovely milk, cream and butter.

CHAPTER SIX
Harvest

$\mathcal{A}$ndy heard it first, he was playing with his horse and cart on the lawn, his sister Betsy was making a crown of daisies for her doll Suki – Suki looked as though she had had measles – she had been left out in the rain and the paint on her face had blistered – when Betsy tried to pat it dry the blister had burst – but Betsy still loved her best and thought she would look pretty with a crown of daisies. She was dropped without ceremony and the daisy crown fell off when Andy suddenly raced across the grass, climbed the gate, shouting its 'Coming, its coming! The threshing machine is coming.' Betsy ran to join him. There was a humming, rumbling and hissing as the great traction engine came into view. There was smoke coming out of its chimney. The fly wheel was spinning so fast you could hardly see it. There was a man with a dusty black face at the steering wheel and another behind him shovelling coal into a furnace. It pulled behind it a huge thing like a wooden house with wheels and belts at various places all over it. The man at the wheel waved to the children and they waved back as they watched it trundle on its way through the village. It was going they knew, to cousin John at Bell Farm and tomorrow they would go there, with their Mum and Dad for a whole day to help with the harvest.

A shaft of sunlight creeping between the half drawn curtains laid a warm finger across Betsy's cheek – she woke, the sunlight filled her eyes, she sat up and remembered; they were going to Bell Farm for the whole day. Seizing Suki whose legs stuck out from under the pillows, she got out of bed, went to the window and leaned out. Some sparrows in a near-by bush were startled and flew off, a cockerel in the farm yard crowed, she could hear the cows who were being milked in the cow shed, their chains about their necks, men shouted and pails clanked.

Amy opened the door and looked round at Betsy's bed, it was empty. 'Betsy', she called. Betsy withdrew her head from the window and ran to her. We are going to Bell Farm today aren't we. 'Yes' said Amy and we had better hurry. Andy is having his breakfast and father will be finished milking anytime now. As she said this she poured water from a jug on the wash stand into the china bowl, pulled off Betsy's nightgown then, threw a towel round her neck and proceeded to wash her face, neck and hands, rubbing her dry, she popped a vest over her head, fastened her liberty bodice and drew on her white Cambric knickers and buttoned them, reached for a blue cotton dress with white frills around the neck and sleeves, turned Betsy round and buttoned up the back.

Washed, dressed, finally her hair brushed, she seized Suki and ran helter skelter down the stairs to join Andy at the table in the big kitchen with a stone floor. Jane Skewes was peeling potatoes at the sink, she wiped her hands on her apron, went to the stove and fetched a large pan of porridge, poured some into a blue china bowl and set it before Betsy – 'quick Jane – treacle and cream she shouted', 'wait a minute, I can't do everything at once' – Jane put the saucepan back on the side of the stove to keep warm then spooned some treacle onto Betsy's porridge and reached over for the cream jug to help herself.

James came with the milk pails full of foaming milk and put them in the adjoining dairy. Jane took a mug, filled it from the pail with warm milk and gave it to Betsy. When she had finished her porridge she buried her nose in the mug and there was white froth on her nose and all round her mouth. She wiped it with the back of her hand. Janie seeing this scolded her and came with a dry towel and wiped her clean.

Andy finished his breakfast first, jumped down from his chair and ran to the back porch where he unearthed a miniature pitch fork from underneath an old mackintosh then took off for the stable yard as fast as his fat little legs would take him. James his father was already putting Sally the chestnut pony between the shafts of the trap and fastening the traces when he had finished and before the bridle was on Andy clambered by way of the metal step at the side, into the trap and sat on the seat facing forward beside where his father would sit. He heaved a contended sigh. This was pride of place!

James finished harnessing Sally, collected various tools, a

pitch fork and heaval and a big tartan rug in case it was cold after the day's work. The evenings were often cold when the sun went down in September. He called out 'Alright Andy?' hold tight and jumped up and sat beside him, flicked the reins and Sally impatient to be off leapt forward.

Sam was mucking out the stables when he heard Sally move off – he ran out and opened the gate and waved to Andy. 'Have a good day and work hard with that pitch fork'. Andy waved back as they went out into the lane and round to the garden gate where Amy and Betsy waited, Betsy clasping Suki tight in her aims. 'Whoa there Sally' crooned James as he pulled her to a halt. Amy and Betsy climbed up and sat on the back seat – back to back with James and Andy. They were off, it was harvest day at Bell Farm. The traction engine was there and lots of people and saffron buns as big as plates.

They arrived, put up Sally in the stable with a hay net and bucket of water, shut and bolted the door.

In the yard called The Mowy, the great engine clattered and groaned – the fly wheel spun so fast you couldn't see it. There were men feeding sheaves of corn from the rick and others pushing it forward into the machine. At the back the grain came in a constant stream and was caught in sacks and carried to the barn.

Friends and neighbours had come and brought helpers. This was an old custom, everyone far and near helped everyone else with their harvest. The children tumbled amongst the straw and men carried sacks of corn into the scrubbed barn and tipped it in a huge heap onto the floor. There was noise and laughter everywhere. You couldn't hear yourself speak.

All the afternoon the thrashing machine and its men, friends and neighbours worked tirelessly. The big rick of corn was reduced to straw and grain. The last sacks were carried to the barn. The last sheaf stacked on a new rick. The whistle blew, the engine stopped. There was a hissing of steam and the fly wheel rotated slowly, slowly until at last it stopped.

From the farmhouse women in pinafores and aprons appeared as if by magic at the sound of the whistle, carrying huge enamel jugs of tea, bowls of sugar and baskets of saffron buns. Everyone gathered round, took a mug from a basket and held it to be filled, then spooned in the sugar and drank the hot sweet tea, letting out gasps of pleasure and wiped their mouths with the back of their hands. There was laughter and back chat – the harvest was in, the sun now in the west began to sink, everybody collected their belongings and children, harnessed ponies to traps and made for home. James and Amy with Andy and Betsy eased their trap into the lane – they too made for home. 'Well' said Amy, 'Some 'ansome day we've 'ad and no mistake, John 'ave turned to farming like a duck takes to water, 'tis five year now since 'ee bought Bell Farm and every one d'love 'im. I been thinking, last week I saw 'im down the cove with Martha – throwing sticks to Shep they was and laughing. I thought, they'm a pretty pair, do you think anything'll come of they two James.' James flicked the reins and Sally quickened her step, 'You'm match making again Amy, let 'em take their time. John ain't in no hurry, let 'im take 'is time. But mind you I shouldn't be surprised, like you say, they'm a pretty pair. E's all'us over to cottage 'an she to the farm.'

They reached the garden gate, Amey and Betsy jumped

down, while James and Andy took Sally and the trap round to the stable yard. Sam was waiting for them. He held Sally's bridle and stroked her nose. "'Ullo my beauty – u'm tired ain't 'ee? Come on then.' and he released the traces and dropped the shafts and led her into the stable. Fresh straw, a fat hay net and a large bucket of cold water awaited her.

Sam patted and crooned to her while he took off her bridle and the rest of her harness. She rubbed her nose against his sleeve – released she went to the bucket and had a long long drink – emerging at last her nose dripping water. Sam put her into her stall, fetched a cloth and rubbed her down, stood a moment and enjoyed her contentment as she pulled at her hay net. 'Goodnight my beauty' he said and slapped lovingly her hind quarters, shut the door and slid the bolt. Harvest day was over for another year.

CHAPTER SEVEN

September

Martha's bedroom window at 'Butterfields' faced east. It got the first rays of the morning sun – the window was wide open, the bottom sash pushed up and the curtains drawn back. It was the last week in September. As the sun crept round the room touching with gold the old furniture and eventually nestling full on Martha's face it woke her. She lay for a few moments blinking at the bright light and the warmth slowly remembering where she was and all that had happened during the week.

Threshing day at Bell Farm – one of the most important days of the year. John Trethewey - he'd bought the farm from her mother five years ago – five years, she said to herself it doesn't seem possible, next week I shall be 24, my birthday and John going on in his thirty's. How time does fly, which reminded her that she had better get up. She had promised herself to go blackberrying now the harvest was over at the farm it was time to make jam and jelly before October set in. It was bad luck to pick blackberries in October.

She yawned, stretched, threw back the bed clothes got out of bed and went to the window, drew back the wisp of curtain that had blown across in the night and leaned out. The sun was up, the air crisp filled with the song rustling and tweeting of birds. A cock crowed and a hen cackled as she laid an egg. A ploughed field was sprinkled with sea gulls looking for worms and in the distance she could hear the waves breaking on the rocks at the end of the meadow. Martha took a deep, deep breath, it felt good to be alive. How lucky to live on the edge of a cliff in Cornwall.

Martha stood at the wash stand and splashed and washed herself, she reached for her brush and brushed her long dark hair, dried herself on a linen towel and pulled on her cambric underwear, her petticoat, blouse – buttoned and with a brooch at the neck, finally her long warm skirt and buttoned boots. She looked at herself in the mirror wondering whether she should tie her hair back with a ribbon or put it up. Tied back would be good for blackberry picking, on the other hand she just might meet John Trethewey. If she put it up she would look grown up! She wanted John to think her grown up. Not always, but mostly, he treated and teased her like she was still a child.

Breakfast finished, the dishes washed and put away. Mother digging in the garden, moving plants and sowing seeds. Martha took a basket and a stout walking stick with a crooked handle and set out for the blackberries that grew all around the hedgerows of Butterfields meadow.

She walked slowly picking as she went, swinging her crooked stick to pull the top branches down within reach, as she neared the cliff top she saw the mine shaft of Trenow Mine, from where she stood she could actually see the blackberries that were growing around the edge of the shaft. There were pickings enough to fill her basket. She walked on down and saw great fat and juicy berries round the edge. Suddenly she became aware of Shep her collie dog, who must have followed her from the cottage, 'Hullo Shep'. You going to pick blackberries, she knelt and patted him and cradled his head against her bosom. Shep reached up and licked her face. She stood up and picked up her basket of berries. As she did so she stepped back. The undergrowth gave way beneath her foot and she was falling, crying out, falling, falling. The basket caught on a branch up ended and spilt the berries. She clutched at the undergrowth thorns and brambles but still was falling, falling. She hit her head on a protruding rock and knew no more.

When Martha opened her eyes, her head ached, she was cold. She wasn't in her bed, where was she. The light was dim, was it night or day? Then, splash – cold water – splash. She opened her eye as George the silly boy from the village was grinning down at her. She tried to move but could not, either her limbs were so hurt or numbed with fright. She heard George a long way off. 'Don't 'ee go for to take fright – you be safe – then no more just blackness. A long, long sleep as she sank once more into unconsciousness.

Five years later, the harvest again. John sitting in a hedge in the stubble field saw Martha now 24 years crossing the far side of the field Shep at her heels picking blackberries. He thinks about their comfortable cottage. The pretty feminine furnishings, the homemade cakes and pies. The little garden full of flowers and Martha. He watches her, sees her in a new light. A woman now but sometimes still a child. Wavy brown hair blowing in the wind, full of golden light. Bleached by the sun to gold, blue eyes, alight with laughter, golden skin and rosy cheeks in the bright sunlight. He had stood on the cliff and watched her, in the cove below, skirt tucked up, bare feet and legs paddling in the surf throwing sticks for Shep. He knew of several young men who would like to wed her – she laughed and joked, danced and flirted with them at the local dances. He wondered why she didn't choose to marry one of them. His thoughts turned to marriage. Bell Farm was big and lonely. He shifted his position in the hedge so that he could keep her in sight. She would make a wonderful wife for any man. The thought flashed through his mind – why not me? Yes, why not. Now I come to think of it, I'm only 35. Five years of hard work behind me. A cow mooed in a nearby field, another answered it. Reminding him of his dairy herd – calves in their pens, sheep on the cliff land and houses – Martha's pets Prince and Lady in the stable – all he needed was company and companionship in his home.

CHAPTER EIGHT
The Mine

So, the harvest was in for another year. The cows were milked and turned out to field. The ducks and hens shut in for the night. John made his way up through the mowy – with its new rick of yellow straw, waiting to be thatched and this year's hay rick. Across the back yard he stopped by the pump to wash his hands and splash his face, put his fingers through his hair, then into the warm kitchen by the back door. He stopped by a mirror on the wall inside the door and combed his wet hair, smoothed it with his hands and thought that will do. He went on into the kitchen, Hilda Thomas who looked after him had left everything clean and tidy. There was a blue check cloth on one end of the table with a tray on which there was a soup bowl and spoon, egg cup and a brown egg waiting to be boiled, a home-made loaf of brown bread and half a pound of yellow home made butter. Hilda saved the cream each day until an enamel bowl was full with a crust settled on the top, then she put it to the side of the kitchen slab until it was simmering hot but not boiled, then she carried it into the dairy to cool. Next day she would churn it into butter, drain off the butter milk and throw in a few handfuls of salt which she later washed off with a pail of fresh water until it tasted just right. The butter milk she saved to make Heavy Cake. Heavy Cake was a speciality in Cornwall. You made a dough like pastry with egg, buttermilk and sultanas, cut candied peel, orange and lemon shredded. Then rolled it out to the size of an oven baking tin, marking it into squares, brushed it with milk and sprinkled sugar all over the top.

John saw to his delight that there was a plate of fresh Heavy Cake. He sat alone at the table and ate his meal.

There was not a sound – just the kettle singing on the slab and his dog Susie snoring a little in her basket.

John thought how quiet the house was – he thought of his cousin James up the valley, his comely wife Amy and their noisy lovely children Andy and Betsy.

The thought struck him like a blow – that is what he needed in this big house, a wife, children to shout and laugh. He boiled his egg and warmed his soup in the pan on the stove and sat alone and ate it, when he had finished he carried the tray to the sink put the pots in a bowl and covered them with water, put the tray against a leg of the kitchen table and took his thumb stick and called to Susie. They would go for a walk before sundown.

The sun was sinking in the west, one of those gold October evenings. They walked through the Mowy out into the field that led to the cove. It was full of stubble made golden by the setting sun. John sat down below a hedge on a mound of grass and Susie sat beside him. In the distance he could see the roof and chimney of Butterfields Cottage. Suddenly the air was rent by a terrifying scream and the barking of a dog. John felt his blood freeze, goose flesh all over him, the dog barked and barked. What the hell's going on he said, 'that's Shep'. – Shep in distress. He got to his feet, called Susie and set off at a run across the field, climbed the hedge. He could see Shep down by the old mine shaft leaping up and down and barking his head off. When John reached Shep he was out of breath and covered in sweat. Shep rushed at him, then back towards the mine shaft, then back to him then, he saw the blackberry basket, caught on a hawthorn branch half full still and spilt blackberries all over the place and about. My god! She's fallen down the shaft – Martha, must have been reaching for berries and over balanced.

John knew that there was a way into the mine from Trenow Beach. The water was always gushing out where there was a cave from which you follow the stream high up into the mine workings. They called it an adit. John started at once into the cave and followed the stream. It was difficult walking and he had to climb up and up by a series of clay ledges. At one point the light went altogether but he felt his way onwards. Susie went in front and helped to guide him by waiting for him on each ledge. At last he came out into the fading light from the sky above the shaft. Martha lay unconscious, blood on her face and hand. Her hair tumbled and wet, he face wet as was her dress and the halfwit George from the village stood above her, his wet cap in his hand. When he saw John he almost collapsed with relief – 'She still alive, she fell down the shaft with her berries. I brought some water in my cap and poured over her, She woke up then went to sleep again.' 'Alright George, don't worry'. Run to the cottage and say I am bringing her home, to warn her Mother – say she must be put her to bed with some milk and honey. George much relieved to be able to escape got into the open, took to his heels and ran.

John knelt beside Martha and gently wiped the blood from her head and face – he dipped his handkerchief in the stream and bathed her forehead and matted hair. After a little while she opened her eyes. John smiled at her 'don't move' he said. 'You're safe now, you'll be alright, I'm going to carry you home'. With that he gathered her up into his arms, waited until she seemed comfortable and not in too much pain. Then started back down the mine – Susie going in front, showing him the way in the dark places with her white tail. At last they were out of the stream. The open air, dusk down, lights twinkling on the distant shore.

Slowly, slowly, painfully he made his way up from the cave and into the meadow. He rested there and leaned against the hedge. He looked down at the little face nesting in his arms and was filled with a protective tenderness like it might have been Susie, only it wasn't Susie it was Martha. Martha who helped him understand Cornish farming, Martha who laughed, put flowers in his parlour, cooked dinners for him, or danced with him at the village social. This was what he wanted, here was his wife, his love, his future.

He stood up from the hedge – held Martha close, felt her heart beating through her thin dress as he made his way across the field to the cottage. Sara was waiting for them.

The door flung wide and the lamp lit, he carried her carefully up the stairs while Sara led the way and held the lamp, he laid her on her bed and stopped and planted a kiss on her forehead. Thinking to himself all the while, when she's quite recovered and we can laugh again, I will ask her if she will marry me. Turning to Sara, keeping his thoughts to himself, he put his arm around her and said 'I guess she'll be alright now – keep her warm and rested – I'll come round tomorrow to see if you need any help, you stay with her. I'll let myself out.

John walked slowly across the field with Susie bounding about him, glad to see him himself again.

CHAPTER NINE
The Rectory

When Mary had made up the fire in Martha's bedroom and taken her tray from her mid day meal down stairs, Martha settled herself comfortably amongst the pillows, watched the flames flickering among the beams of the old ceiling as the fresh logs began a fitful blaze. Her thoughts slipped to the past and she dozed. She was abruptly woken by a bad dream – she was wet, cold, hurt, lying on the ground in the old mine and the idiot boy George was leaning over her – she woke with a start, a silent scream on her lips. No sound came, she could not cry out – her night gown was wet with sweat, she started up afraid – then she remembered. She was in her own room, safe in the old four poster, she pushed back the damp hair from her forehead and sank back on to her pillows. She remembered, John came, her John, John Trethewey – he put his arms around her and held her close. Telling her gently that everything was alright – that she was safe, then gathering her up in his strong arms carried her out of the mine and across the fields to her home Butterfield Meadow. George had done as John bid him and ran to tell her mother. Her Mother was waiting – a hot bottle in her bed and a warm shawl to wrap her in. John had whispered to her, held her close and fondled her and then safe in her bed, she had slept. Now, closing her eyes, her thoughts searched the past. She had spent a few days in bed, when she was better John came and had tea with her in the new kitchen – it was dusk – the pink lamp was lit, next day he came again and asked her if she was strong enough to go for a walk. It was a golden day at the end of October. They walked to the cove, little wavelets were breaking on the shingle and the pebbles rattled as they receded. The little waves came again whispering to the pebbles who chattered back to them as they receded again. John skimmed flat stones so skilfully, the sea gulls rocking gentle on the ripples, flew up went a little further away to escape – they lingered John holding her hand. The sun was a huge red ball of fire on the horizon. The sky all streaked with crimson and gold. They sat on the rocks and watched the sun sink down below the grey horizon – the sky had turned from blue to gold, now indigo. The edge of a silver moon just began to show above the headland.

John put his arm about Martha's shoulder, drew her slowly towards him, she looked up at him and smiled, he kissed her full on the lips. Smiling down at her he said 'Martha will you marry me and come home to Bell Farm?' In her mind's eye she saw it all so vividly as she remembered.

They were married in the ancient church which stood above the sea on the hill above Lansallo Cove. She wore her white muslin dress with a white satin sash – it had a big bow at the back and reached to the hem. The one she had worn for her confirmation, it had lain wrapt in tissue paper in a cardboard box in the bottom of the oak press ever since.

All the village were there – Aunt Mary helping with the feast at Bell Farm. Uncle Joel gave her away and the Parson was so good and kind. There was holly and ivy to decorate the church and sheaves of corn at the door and round the pulpit. Sara stopped thinking about the wedding – her mind raced on.

They lived together at Bell Farm – it was wonderful – the old house refurbished – leaking windows replaced, new chintzes and curtains and John found at a sale an old four poster bed, mended it himself, a new mattress and rosy chintz curtains and covers. There was a lump in her throat and a few tears squeezed out and ran down onto her pillow. She brushed them away with the back of her hand and sniffed hard. Oh! What memories she thought.

Mary was born just before Christmas the following year and baptized at the carol service on Christmas Eve – they had been blissfully happy – the harvest came and went. Martha thought nothing could touch their happiness in this idyllic remote spot on the Cornish coast. She stirred in her bed restlessly and coughed as she remembered what had happened to bring it all to an abrupt end.

There was a band of fishermen dabbling in the smuggling trade across the channel with France – the slight danger and excitement caught at John's imagination and anyway one could not be detected in such an out of the way place – he joined in, enjoyed it – but there were always those who were malicious, who delighted in telling tales and saying 'don't say as I said, mind'. The fisherman, arranged to land a cargo on Christmas Eve – believing the authorities would be busy with Christmas at home – John was there amongst them. The Excise men got to hear of it and were waiting – as they neared the shore their muskets rang out – the cargo dumped – men scattered in the undergrowth – John, her John – the tears flowed down her cheeks again – was shot in the leg – there was a hue and cry all over the village – Mary was just six years old. A man had come pounding on the door telling Martha to come at once – bring a bowl, water and cloth to the church – John was hit in the leg and Parson had locked them in the church for safety. She felt cold with gooseflesh as she remembered. What did she do. She took Mary from her bed wrapped her in a cloak – collected a bowl of hot water and old linen together Mary clinging to her skirt, they had gone to the church. Parson was waiting for them and locked the door behind them. She could see it all now – John on the floor, blood oozing from his leg wound, Parson holding a candle – Ned and Joe Semmens trying to stem the blood ''E 'vet got a bullet in his leg' Joe said, 'Us got to get 'im out' he produced a knife – he used to clean fish and handed it to her – it was dirty she remembered and put it in the water and wiped it on a bit of linen, as she relived the moment her throat went dry. She had nearly fainted at the time and John? He cried out something awful – she held his leg felt the bullet a lump under the flesh of his calf and plunged the knife carefully in and cut the flesh away and there it was a round musket bullet – it was out – Ned held John's head to smother his cries – she washed the wound as best she could – the Excise men were shouting in the church yard. Parson blew out the candle. She pulled the wound together with her fingers and bound it tight. When all was done they waited, held their breath till the hullabaloo outside quietened down. They must have waited an hour – it seemed to Sara an eternity at last all was quiet – Martha took off her cloak and they wrapped John in it. Ned spoke in a horse whisper 'What us g'un do Joe'. Joe said 'Take un over to France – they'll look after 'ee'. ''Ess' said 'Ned, we best do that now. Come on Joe lift um up'. So that was what they did – Sara wept silently into her pillow – she hadn't seen him since and now Mary was a grown woman eighteen years this Christmas – she rolled over and buried her face in the pillow. It was Christmas Eve again – she slept – the opening of the door awoke her – it was Mary with a tray of tea.

It was Christmas Eve.

Mary Trethewey stood beside the washing up bowl and leant against the table which stood in front of the big lattice window – her hands resting idle in the water, hardly feeling the cloth which floated from her fingers.

At eighteen her body was just beginning to show the rounded curves of adolescence. She was lost in the memories of her childhood.

Nothing had been the same since the fateful Christmas Eve twelve years ago, when her father had lain sick and wounded in the church, a bullet in his leg. He had been caught by a surprise attack of the Excise men. Lost in her reverie she leant forward and peered through the lattice at the sea beyond the headland. It was grey and very cold. White horses leapt and chased each other across the open bay. Down in the cove it would be sheltered – the cove being shaped like a horse shoe, would have its back to the wind.

Mary thought back to the days when she lived at Bell Farm. So called because of the great bell mounted on one end of the roof of the barn to give warning of ships in distress. A sudden gust of wind rattled the lattice and recalled her to her surroundings, she felt guilty, the water was cold. There was much to do. Since the disappearance of her father, she and her mother had lived at the Rectory, where her mother had been for the last ten years, housekeeper to the widowed Rector.

She finished the washing up, making a mental note of all there was to do that afternoon. As her mother had failed in health, Mary had taken more upon herself. There was the ham to remove from the saucepan and stick with cloves, a Christmas ritual she loved, afterwards smearing it with thick brown sugar and pouring over it a cup of rough cider before placing it in the oven to roast.

Many a year, she had leant over the big oak table, waiting for the moment when her mother fetched the jar of cloves and let her stick them in, carefully making little patterns as she did so. Once she made a picture of a pig and afterwards, when it was in the oven, she felt sorry for the pig and could not eat her bacon.

These little memories flitted through her mind as she performed her tasks. Her mother lay upstairs in bed, Mary heard her cough, a chill had settled on her chest, making her weak and listless. She would run up to see if she wanted anything and make her comfortable before going over to the church to clean up after the decorators. It was her job to set the new white candles for the midnight mass in their shining sockets. After that, if there was time, she would run down to the cove.

The back staircase was old and dark, as Mary climbed the worn treads, they creaked and groaned at every step. The wind howled and hurled itself at the old walls. Snatching at the latch of the little window on the half landing, as tho' it would enter and catch her round the corner. She felt a sudden premonition, whether for good or bad, she could not say. She heard her mother coughing again – she shivered and hurried on.

Mrs Trethewey lay in the big four poster that had been her marriage bed at Bell Farm. She looked very small and frail. It was a big shadowy room under the eaves and over the kitchen. Mary's heart smote her and the feeling of foreboding returned – was this just a chill? Or was it something more? Was her mother gradually letting go of life, as hope for the return of the husband she loved, faded?

Mary always kept a fire of driftwood burning on the hearth in her mother's room when the east wind was blowing, she went forward now and stirred the embers with the toe of her boot, flames leapt up as she kicked the logs, flooding the room with dancing light and throwing great shadows, that leapt about among the smoky rafters. It was warm, the air thick with wood smoke, the smell of bacon drifted up from the kitchen below.

Mary went over and took the limp hand that lay on the coverlet between her warm brown ones and chafed it, a lump rose in her throat, to feel her mother's hand so frail, which had once been so strong at the butter churn.

'I've set the bacon to roast Mother', she said, 'and when I've taken 'er out of the oven, I be going to sweep the church, do'ee want for anything a'fore I go as I be going to run down to the cove for a breath of fresh air when I've finished?'

Mrs Trethewey smiled and shook her head. 'No dear', she said, 'do'ee run down to the cove then, but mind 'ow 'ee do go, 'tis some slippery this time 'year'.

Mary squeezed her hand and kissed her "Es mother I'll mind', 'do 'ee 'ave a sleep now and I'll be back'. Mrs Trethewey smiled a tired smile and returned the squeeze.

Mary leant on her broom in the dim church, all about her was a green bower of holly and ivy – the air heavy with the scent of damp moss piled high on the window ledges – and the thick sweet smell of wax from many candles, long since burnt away. At her feet lay a pile of sweepings – moss and little springs of holly discarded by the village women whose chatter, gossip and laughter had echoed round the stone pillars and called back to them from the vaulted roof a few hours ago.

Lansallo Church had once been a monastery – the pews, hand carved from solid logs of wood, stand to this day. It was sparsely furnished on account of its great size, and made the stranger wonder to see such a great church nestling in a small hamlet just above the sea. The pigeons who once nested in the dove cot in the Rectory garden, now made do with the draughty belfry, murmured, and rearranged themselves – the gulls cried as they sailed by on the wind.

It was getting dark, Mary knew she would have to hurry if she wanted to go to the cove. Reaching for the dust pan and sweeping up the little pile of leaves, she spied several sprigs of holly that smiled at her with their shiny red berries as if to say 'Don't throw us away'. She knelt down, and gathered them together, planning to surprise her mother by decorating her room and the old kitchen. There were several good strands of ivy and here was a sprig of rosemary. Carefully she extricated it from the pile of rubbish, pinched it between her finger and thumb and held it to her nose. 'Rosemary for remembrance', she said aloud and thought about her father.

Here in this church it had happened twelve years ago. Yes! There he had lain, over by the old cupboard that held the vestments. She could remember it all quite clearly. Somehow she had never given it any great thought, dismissing the scene from her mind as part of the world of grown up people. Now she felt as tho' it was happening again. A shiver ran over her, someone was walking over her grave!

She peered among the shadowy pews and pillars, frightened at what she might see.

What was that? Over by the door? Was that the wind that tried to lift the latch, rustling among the thick plush curtains like a muffled football – or was it Jo Semmens and his brother Ned come to fetch her father away. She was a child of six again, crouching where her mother had put her, in a great dark pew, perched on a hassock with a sharp button cutting into her little buttocks, not daring to move, lest worse befall her father. He so handsome and strong who could shoulder any burden that others failed to bear, now brought low with a wound in his leg. Jo Semmens, a fisherman , had fetched her mother and after much whispering and gathering together of old linen and a bowl of water hid under a cloak they had made their way to the side entrance of the church. She had been bundled into a pew and told to hide there, not to look out or make a sound. Jo had said the Excise men were all over the countryside looking for father. Her mother had taken the bullet from his leg and father had cried out – the pain must have been mortal bad. She had stuffed her fat little fingers in her ears to shut out the sound, a great sob shook her and the tears had run silently down her rosy cheeks and into her mouth. There was no handkerchief in her pocket so she had wiped her nose on her rough sleeve and her face had been sticky. Then he had gone quiet. Ned Semmens had joined his brother and stealing like shadows down the aisle, together they had borne him away. Her mother said he had gone to France and would come home again one day. The rusty working of the belfry clock suddenly set up a growling as they gathered their strength to strike the hour, giving her quite a start and recalling her to her surroundings.

Mary hurriedly set aside her gleanings and swept the rubbish into the pan and dusted a few drops of water off a book rest. She could hear her heart beating when the clock stopped striking, one, two, three, four. It was in fear and trembling that she hurried down the shadowy aisle to the vestry, to fetch the new candles she must place upon the altar.

Pushing open the vestry door she hesitated, holding her breath as the silent dark looked back at her. The cassocks on their hooks looked like ghosts and seemed to say 'Hurry, Mary, Hurry'. She fumbled with the heavy lid of the chest where the candles were kept, dropping it and pinching her finger – she cried out and the echo mocked her long after she had finished sucking it. She got the candles out at last and hurried with them to the altar, where the gleaming brass candlesticks – so carefully tended by Mrs Hobbs gnarled old hands, were waiting to receive them.

Mary laid the candles down and crossed herself, then carefully fitted them into their sockets, fascinated to watch the thin curls of white wax appear like lace round the base of each as she pressed them down to fit. The great vases on the altar were filled with holly, rosemary and Christmas roses white as wax. She looked at them and then at the great crucifix in the centre from which Jesus hung the crown of thorns about his head, only a loin cloth to cover his nakedness – she thought how cold he must be and shivered. Looking again at the vases of holly it occurred to her that even the symbols of Christmas like the holly with its sharp prickles, that had so often drawn blood from her childish fingers had pointed at the crown of thorn and the blood he must shed. She thought of her first communion last Easter – the Rector's words as he held the silver cup high over her head.

'The blood of our Lord Jesus Christ, which was shed for Thee'.

She felt as tho' it had indeed been shed for her, as if it was all her fault. She looked again at the worn figure wasted with pain and suddenly thought of her mother. Her mother looked like this, pale and worn with a terrible look of resignation on her face.

'She's going to die!' thought Mary, 'She wants to die!' In panic Mary knelt at the altar and raised her eyes to Christ. 'Don't let her die', she prayed, 'please don't let her die.' She didn't stop to think how hopeless it might be – she just prayed as she had never prayed before. 'Send father back to us. Don't let my mother die'. The hot tears welled up and filled her eyes, overflowed down her cheeks scalding them and dripped on to her clasped hands. She opened her eyes and saw through a haze of tears, the face of Our Lord looking down at her. He seemed to smile and say 'Don't cry Mary'. Go home. Your mother needs you. All will be well. All will be well'. She heard those words, heard them with her own ears – heard the whisper in the wind, 'all will be well, all will be well'. She brushed the tears from her eyes the better to see his smile, but he was just as before, cold and sad.

Mary was cold, she jumped to her feet and hurried to her brush and pan, the sprigs of holly and Rosemary beside it. She emptied the pan and put it with the brush behind the fearful vestry door now no longer fearful – knowing as she did that he was beside her. She closed the door and tiptoed back between the garlanded pillars and swung open the heavy outer door. The cold east wind blew in from the sea, gathered her up by catching a corner of her cloak as if to help her along.

Down the path and through the gate into the village she ran, the bunch of holly held aloft to balance herself as she skipped the puddles. The rusty clock in the belfry tower struck five – it was already dusk. Mary realised it was now too late to go to the cove but she didn't care – there was only one thought in her head, to rush home and tell her mother. She sped up the garden path – pushed open the heavy studded door, the east wind rushing in behind her and slammed it – she leant against it panting and laughing, all her fears forgotten.

On a shelf in the scullery stood a neat row of candlesticks, china, brass and silver for the parlour, each had a new white candle in it. Mary took a taper from a jar on the kitchen

mantle, after lighting it at the stove she lit the row of candles, whose lights all jumping up out of the darkness made strange shadows. The bunch of onions hanging from the ceiling, looked like a man dangling from a gibbet and swayed a little in the draught from the cracked scullery window. While the cider barrel with the bung in it looked like a giant gnome.

She must hurry, the Rector would have finished writing his sermon which was never very long on account of all the Christmas dinners waiting to be eaten. She selected a candle in a gleaming silver candlestick which always stood on a side table by his elbow chair.

Mary knocked at the parlour door and entered. The Rector was slumped in his chair before the dying embers and must have been dozing. She set the candle on the table by his side and knelt to rake the fire together, blowing the red ash and coaxing it to a blaze before putting on fresh wood and fir cones from the basket beside the hearth.

The Rector sat upright and ran his bony fingers through his thin silver hair – while Mary drew the heavy brown velvet curtains, stiff on their old rings. They had hung in the parlour ever since she could remember and many's the time she had stayed behind after her mother's dusting was finished, playing at keeping house behind their folds, singing little songs to her dolls.

'How's your mother, Mary?' he said in his gruff rather abrupt voice, drawing his silver brows together over his sharp old eyes, in a manner which had often struck terror to an erring choir boy or wrong doer, but which she was quite accustomed to since she had lived in his house for the past twelve years.

'She ain't no better nor no worse Sir, thank 'ee kindly. She do cough same as ever – but it do come to me this arternoon when I were sweeping the church that it ain't neither a chill nor a cough as be the real trouble. ''Tis me father as be troubling 'er'. The Rector peered closely at her. There was a look of maturity about her these days since her mother took to her bed and she had taken over the running of the house with the deftness and capability of a far older woman.

He looked at her now, gazing as she was intently into the fire. He noticed the roundness of her figure and the comeliness of her rosy cheeks, lit by the gentle light from the blazing logs and flickering candle. Mary is grown up he thought. He must question her to see what was in her mind – he did not know how much she remembered of that fateful Christmas Eve, or had been told by her mother.

No one knew more than he the ache in Martha's heart all these years. It was he who had met Jo Semmens fleeing with the nigh unconscious man in his arms, dragging the wounded leg – the Excise men calling after them and swinging their lanterns round every bush in their search.

The Excise men had surprised the little band of local smugglers led by John Trethewey in the cove at the foot of Bell Farm, landing a cargo of Brandy and a few bundles of silks and lace. Christmas Eve had been chosen as it was to be supposed that the preventative officers would be busy at home with their women folk. But not so – their boats had been sighted before they could reach the shelter of the rocks and word had gone round. The kegs had been dumped in the sea and the bundles stored in a hole in the cliff face almost invisible to the unknowing eye. John had stayed till last making all safe while his men scattered into the darkness of the cliff. As the bullet hit him in the left leg, Jo Semmens saw him fall on the steep path below the fields. John had gone back at once and dragged him into the undergrowth, where they had lain low till the hue and dry about the cove had died down. He had had to stifle John's groans with his woollen cap. When he had thought it safe to move he had half carried half dragged the nigh unconscious man up the path and over the two fields to the village – before they could reach the farm the Rector had met them as he left the church after preparing for the midnight mass. Realising what was afoot, he had seized Jo by the arm and half pushed half dragged them into the church yard where they sank down upon a grave stone while he unlocked the church door. Between them they lifted and dragged the injured man into the safety of the church whose peace and quiet received them as he shut and bolted the door. He went to the vestry and lit a candle, advancing with it held high above his head, the better to see who they were and what was the matter. The candle had made a halo round his silver hair as he stood in the middle of the main aisle. 'Sanctuary' he said in a strong fierce voice and crossed himself. 'Amen!' said Jo pulling the woollen cap from his head and feeling that he was in the presence of the Almighty himself. 'Come with me' he had said 'and we will fetch Martha, his wife.'

The soft closing of the door disturbed him. He recalled himself with a jolt. He was getting old he supposed. Mary had gone to fetch the tea. He was dreaming. He got up and collected the scattered papers on his desk that held his sermon for Christmas Day. 'Peace on earth, goodwill towards men'. That was his text.

It always was at Christmas – what matter, it could never grow old and perhaps if it was preached from every pulpit till the end of time it might come to pass, men stop their petty quarrels on earth and look to the greater life to come.

His joints felt stiff, he thought the greater life would not be far off for himself. He wondered what Mary had meant when she said that her mother had been afflicted by her father more than the cough or cold. How brave Martha had been when he had persuaded her to leave Bell Farm and become his house keeper. The farm and contents had sold well – Martha Trethewey had enjoyed a modest independence besides the shelter of his roof, which had kept over-zealous government officials at bay, who might otherwise have pestered her with questions as to the whereabouts of her husband. Ah well! That was a long time ago and he supposed that no one thought of it now but the three occupants of his own house. Martha, Mary her daughter and he who had taken upon himself to play so great a part in their tragedy.

As he stood before the blazing logs he suddenly straightened himself to his full height. 'I will answer to the greatest shepherd of all for the protection of my flock' he said.

'Did you speak Sir?' said Mary returning with the tea tray. 'No Mary, I was only talking to myself. Thinking aloud if you like'.

Mary settled him into his favourite chair and drew the table close to his elbow. There were hot buttered scones and saffron cake. She poured out a steaming cup of tea and handed it to him. He took it and sank back against his cushion, in his heart, thanking God for these two good women who had taken such care of him. He became aware that Mary had not left the room but was busying about. 'What are you doing Mary? Your mother will be wanting you.' 'Oh no Sir, 'tis alright, I be just going to her – but 'ave a few sprigs of holly for 'ee! I picked they up in the Church, it was a shame to leave they and they smiling up at me, as t'were asking me to take 'em and use 'em'.

As she spoke she moved deftly about the small pictures that hung around the mantelshelf and fixed a tiny sprig above each. 'Now! Do'ee look – ain't that a bit more like Christmas 'ave really come? I 'ave a bit more for me mother and a bit for the kitchen, and . . .' she fumbled in the folds of the bodice of her dress. 'I 'ave a sprig of Rosemary for remembrance.' She held it out for him to see. 'I'm going to give this to me mother in the morning along with a shawl I've knitted for 'er'. With that she broke off an unsightly twig at the bottom of the spray and threw it into the fire. The flames leapt up and a sweet aroma like incense stole into the room with the wood smoke.

'Ah well! I'll be going to me mother now' she said – 'If you 'ave all you d'need Sir? Don't 'ee go out no more till the service. 'Tis a bitter east wind getting up and the sea is calling for a storm'. With that she moved to the door with a soft firm tread and closed it gently behind her.

Mary entered her mother's room struggling a little with the heavy tray she had prepared for the two of them and set it on a table by the fire. Her mother had lit her bedside candle. The room was warm and smoky, filled with a gentle light. Martha lay pale and sad, she seemed far away and reluctant to bring her mind to the tea. Mary crossed over to her a steaming cup in one hand and buttered scones in the other. 'Now do 'ee sit up a bit Mother' she said, setting down the cup and plate and helping her to raise herself, plumping up the pillows and tidying the coverlet. Martha smiled up at her and said 'Your Father is very near me today, perhaps the good Lord 'ave taken 'im these past years and its me the one trying to believe him alive. If 'tis so perhaps he means to take me soon, for I feel that we are very near and like to meet again'. Mary flung herself down beside the bed. 'No no Mother, 'tisn't so, 'tisn't so, I spoke with the dear Lord this 'arternoon in the church, Father's coming home, that's what 'ee said, I know it, I feel it'. She bent her head and sobbed, pouring out to her mother all the fears and feelings she had had in the church during the afternoon. Martha stretched out a hand and stroked the dark hair tumbled over the white coverlet.

'There! There!' she said, 'don't 'ee go for to cry. If 'tis the Lord's wish to take me – and John Trethewey and I do meet again 'twill be the happiest moment of my life. Come drink your tea child 'tis getting cold.'

Mary got up and flung back the dark hair, scraping the wisps off her wet cheeks with her little brown fingers. 'Don't talk so' she said. ''Tis my belief you'm thinking yourself into your grave – 'tis me father – if 'ee be dead why can't he let us be?'. She fetched her cup and plate, sat on a stool by the bedside and took a great bite from a hot buttered scone. The melting butter escape and dripped down her chin, she licked it off with her tongue and sniffed away the remains of the tears. 'You and me's been 'appy enough Mother dear' she said, leaning forward urgently to emphasise her words, as tho' that would make it true. You'm a gert strong woman yet. You'm little I know! If you've a mind to you could be up tomorrow. 'Tis not the cold that's getting 'ee – 'tis the poor spirit that's got into 'ee these last weeks, do 'ee forget about me father mother dear, leave us let um bide with the Lord if so 'ee's called um 'ome. 'Ave some of this 'ere saffron cake and see ef I can make as good as you'. With that she cut the cake, a thick slice for herself and a small one for her mother. They ate in silence for a while. Mary could see that Martha's thoughts had strayed again – she ate slowly and her gaze was ever drawn to the lattice.

Mary finished her cake and washed it down with the scalding tea – it tasted good and comforting, she felt a whole heap better with some warm food inside her – all this spirited stuff was not for her. 'Twas Christmas Eve! There were many things to do before the midnight mass. She gathered up the tray and clattered down the stairs with it, humming a bit of 'Hark the Herald Angels Sing' as she went. There would be carol singers presently – her miniature bosom swelled with pride and she felt her bodice grow tight, as she thought of handing round mince pieces made by her own hands. She thought of the larder shelves almost as full of good things as if her mother was well – pies and puddings tied in white cloths, creams and sweetmeats, lemon curd into which she loved to dip her fingers.

Outside the wind was rising. Jo Semmens pulled on his oilskins and great boots, thinking it would be as well to go down to the cove and see that the boats were secure. He often did a bit of fishing in winter when weather permitted. The few fish that he caught helped with the meagre diet of the villagers – the miners from Wheal Grace in particular. Their lot was poor he knew – if it was a long winter and not more than one wreck to tide them over. They relied poor souls on the pickings from a good wreck and what poor flotsam and jetsam the sea had to offer. The fisher folk didn't do so badly, they were rewarded in kind by the farming folk, who were glad of a bit of fish to relieve the monotony of their diet, but not always so the miners. He turned to look at the chimney of Wheal Grace, standing tall and stark against the scudding clouds, every now and then illuminated by a fitful moon. A figure detached itself from the shadows, it was his brother Ned. The thunder of the surf reached their ears as they neared the cove. The tide was out, the boats lay quiet, high upon the shingle – they climbed the stile and made their way down to the beach – felt the ropes in turn and examined their fastenings – went a little further to see where the last tide had left its tell tale line of seaweed and shells. 'If we don't get proper gale they will be safe enough' Ned shouted, ''Es' Jo bellowed back. They scanned the sea, the moon shone fitfully and they could see nothing. 'Us better be getting back' shouted Jo. 'Time's getting on I got to go to church direcly!' He was verger as well as sextant and he had his job at Church to see to – books to be put out in the pews and candles to light. The bell to toll. 'Christmas be 'ere again' he shouted – ''Es' came the reply. ''Ee do soon come round. Do 'ee mind that Christmas Eve that 'ee brought up John Trethewey' shouted Ned. They were climbing the steep path now that led in slippery ledges to the two fields above. 'Ah!' said Jo. 'Do 'ee mind Ned that night as we carried 'ee down this 'ere path unconscious and put um in the boat covered um with the tarpaulin and took it out put um aboard that there French cutter. I do often wonder what's happened to John'. They walked abreast now through the two fields that led to the church and the village nestling behind it as if for shelter. Ned stopped and looked up at the big bell on the end of the barn at Bell Farm. 'I reckon as John Trethewey would have been reading the lesson and handing the plate tonight if 'ee'd been 'ere' said Jo, ''ess I reckon so', said Ned. 'Come on Jo, supper will be waiting. Missus will be fidgeting, she got to get cleared before the service'. The two men parted by the church and went their ways to their cottages.

Jo opened the door and went in – the light from three candles smote him after the dark night. 'You got a brave bit o'light here Mother' he called. 'Oh Jo is that you' called Annie his wife. 'I be just coming – supper's ready – take off your boots – 'ess it is nice to 'ave a bit of light on Christmas Eve – you d know well 'ow I like to light they candles.'

Annie put a great bowl of stew on the table an called up the stairs to her children. There came the sound of a minor stampede and two tousled children, a boy and a girl, appeared at the foot of the stairs and joined them at the table. Ruan the elder like his father, tall and well built for his twelve years, with ruddy cheeks and dark hair. Loveday was nine, fair like her mother and shy. Annie ladled out the stew into huge soup plates and Jo cut the loaf and gave a thick square of bread to each. Then they sat and ate in silence, wrapped about by the warm glow of fire and candle light. They always ate hearty on Christmas Eve to keep the cold out.

Meanwhile Mary had sped on winged feet. The stove was packed with wood, the old oak table was laid at one end for herself and the Parson with a crisp white cloth and blue china. A plate of mince pies was set by the stove to warm and a great brown earthenware jug of cider stood with many things at the other end of the table, ready to welcome the carol singers. There was the ham stuck with cloves and a new crusty loaf made by her own hands. A tray laid ready for her mother held a little junket in a rosy dish, topped with jam and clotted cream. Mary's face was flushed and happy, and her heart was full of gladness as she completed her preparations. Lastly, the moment she had been waiting for! She fetched the remaining sprigs of holly and deftly arranged them behind the little pictures beside and above the mantelshelf. There was a picture of a donkey leaning over an orchard gate, talking to some geese. She stopped and looked at it, How happy they were, instead of being trussed up in a roasting tin like the one she had just stuffed with onions and put in the larder, a bowl of apple sauce for company. She sighed and climbed onto a chair to lay a few sprigs of holly among the ornaments and two china dogs that gazed unseeingly back at her. Here was her favourite, a ship in a storm, painted on glass – how brave the sailors were, she said a little prayer in her heart and hoped too many were not on the sea that night. She looked towards the window – it was closed, the shutters barred. The chintz curtains lay gay and tranquil and the sound of the wind was afar off.

Suddenly another sound broke the stillness of the night – the click of the gate and shuffle of many boots – the carol singers were here. Mary sped on winged feet down the passage to the parlour. 'Parson! Parson, the carol singers be come, do 'ee come quickly and let um in!'

The old man raised his hands to his disordered silver hair

and shuffled to his feet – hastening after her down the passage he unbarred the great kitchen door. In they came! Rough men, young boys, farm lads and comely girls – crowding about the stove – snatching off their caps and calling a Merry Christmas. As they took their stand an old man with a rosy face and a merry twinkling eyes stepped forward and sounded a note. The most beautiful sound Mary had ever heard broke forth 'While shepherds watch their flocks by night' – sung in parts as only Cornishmen know how – 'All seated on the ground. The Angel of the Lord came down and glory shone around.'

Mary was wrapped in a glory of sound and sight of light and warmth of body and mind – scrambling to her feet she ran upstairs to her mother – flinging the door wide that her mother might share the beautiful music and feel the spirit of Christmas that had entered the house. She sat on the stairs and listened halfway between the singers and her mother, that she might be the bond between them. Her heart beat wildly too full of joy to think. She could only feel and breathe and listen. The carol came to its end. The voices below murmured among themselves. A boy's treble was raised in 'Silent Night, Holy Night' – she knew who that would be – it was Johnnie Hoskin – she crept down the stairs and peeped round the corner to watch him as he sang. His fair hair clustering about his face, which was raised to the smoky ceiling, as tho' he saw his maker and sang only for him. Some said his maker would call him before his time. Mary examined him as he sang and thought his legs looked sturdy enough for all his angelic pale face. So carol followed carol.

When the singing came at last to a close Mary darted forward into the kitchen, seized the plate of mince pies from the stove and began handing them round exchanging happy greetings with them all. The Rector told Charlie Jordan to pour out the cider – a tall dark boy of eighteen was Charlie – with a skin tanned gold by the sun and wind. He was the farmer's son from Bell Farm. Alf Jordan his father, had bought the farm when Martha had sold it. Mary and Charlie had been good friends in school but had not met much of late as Charlie worked from dawn till dusk with his father and Mary was kept in the house by her extra duties. She blushed now – the hot blood burning her breasts and flushing her cheeks – as he offered her a mug of cider. She laughed up at him with merry eyes. 'Exchange ain't no robbery' she said gaily and offered him a pie. He too felt a little confusion and bit deep into his pie to hide it, filling his mouth with crisp pastry and mincemeat till it oozed out at the corners and he could not reply. He munched and swallowed and drew breath. 'Going to church d'reckley r'ee' he asked. ''Ess' said Mary, 'Ar' you?' ''Ess!' came the reply, he leant forward as if to emphasise the importance of his words. 'Shall I see you 'ome after?' Mary blushed deeply and laughed with her merry eyes, 'Alright ef you've a mind to' she said. They were interrupted by old Tom the postman who was collecting them all together as it was time to move on. Charlie suddenly put down his mug seized her hand and squeezed it. She couldn't squeeze back, it was so sudden. His hand burnt her and the burn travelled up her arm and all over her body. 'Thank you' was all she said. Then he was gone – out into the night with all the others – she heard the shuffle of their feet and the click of the gate.

'Don't 'ee go back to the parlour Parson' she called, 'we'm best have out supper now. Do 'ee cut the bacon slices, while I take this tray to me mother'. Off she went with the tray nimble as a cat and as light of foot, up the dark back stairs to the room above. Martha looked flushed, Mary hoped she hadn't fever, setting down the tray Mary felt her head. ''Tis not me head hear that is bad it is me heart'. Mary didn't understand, but thought the music and singing had excited her. 'Eat your supper then 'twill do you good – Parson is below cutting the bacon, after supper it will be time for church. I must fly and no mistake'. With that she sped back down the stairs.

The warmth of the kitchen – the good ham and the crusty bread and most of all the home brewed cider made Mary feel full of happiness and well being. She played the old game of 'he loves me he loves me not' with the clovers around the plate and thought of Charlie. The thought made her blush again and she felt hot when she remembered the squeeze of his hand. 'A believe 'ee do love me' she thought and the thought pleased her. She smiled gently to herself unaware that the kindly old man at the end of the table watched her from beneath his shaggy brows and guessed her thoughts. It pleased him to think that she and Charlie might become sweethearts, she like a velvety flower on a tender stalk. He as straight and upstanding as a sapling, as fine a young farmer as you could see for many a mile around.

Straight as a die, a good churchman too – many's the time he had scythed the churchyard or tolled the bell when an older man was sick. Yes it pleased him. If anything should happen to Martha, Mary would be left in his care. What could be more suitable for her, than to become the wife of Charlie Jordan, and go home as a bride to the home of her forefathers. He puffed his pipe while Mary washed the dishes – he too felt warm and at peace with all men.

'there Parson she called 'I've nearly finished, do 'ee put your top coat on for church and wrap a scarf around your 'at and 'ead. 'Tis some cold tonight. The wind be still rising 'tis calling for a storm for sure. I 'ope we don't get no rain afore we gets back from the service.' With that she dried her hands and undid her apron. 'I'll see me mother now and fetch me cloak'. The Parson fetched his heavy black coat, broad brimmed hat and scarf which according to her bidding he wound about his head and neck – it would at least keep his hat on he thought.

Mary was soon back, her green freeze cloak wrapped all about her. The hood drawn over her head and turned back to show the red lining – it reminded him of the holly and he thought what a Christmas picture she was.

Parson lifted the latch and tugged open the door, together they bent their heads to meet the wind. As they crossed the dark yard and into the street, Parson took her arm with a protective gesture – but partly to steady himself over the rough places. She, sensing this, braced herself to be his aid should he trip or his steps falter, so each, the old man and the young girl gave to each other the help that they needed. They could see the light shining from the open church door as they crossed the street. Other figures emerged from the shadows – the cottage windows were all ablaze. Voices called greetings to them and each other as they all converged on the church. Some had come by pony trap or gig and the horses could be heard stamping and whinnying where they were tethered. The midnight mass was always well attended, country folk came from far and near.

Parson let go her arm as they entered the porch – she stood back to let him go forward and enter alone. There were many people already in their places. Some sitting whispering, some devoutly kneeling, praying some special prayer. Mary slipped into her pew wondering what they prayed.

Jo Semmens was there, his great black boots showing below his cassock, lighting all the candles that stood in iron stands at the end of all the pews, tonight wreathed in ivy. The altar was already a blaze of light and the warm smell of human bodies mingled with that of warm damp moss and bunches of Rosemary on the window ledges. She felt safe and happy and wished her mother were here. Yes! – that was her special prayer at Christmas – that her father be sent home and her mother not taken from her. She drew out the threadbare hassock and knelt upon it, covered her face with her hands till the end of her fingers were white with the perseverance of her prayer.

The Parson began to intone the first prayers, his voice firm and clear rose and fell with the beautiful words – Mary hemmed in on all sides by her friends and neighbours felt warm and secure. The wind might howl and buffet the windows but inside was light, warmth and radiance, here was Christmas itself. The service continued, the voices about her rose and fell, Mary forgot all else in the wonder of it.

Ned Semmens was not a great churchman like his brother, he pleased himself – went his way expecting others to treat him as he treated them fairly without sentiment or fuss. He was a fisherman like his brother Jo. He thought 'Ef the Good Lord was above, some said 'e was Jo for one'. Then 'e s'posed 'e would take care of 'e ef 'e lived right. But he didn't hold with no fuss and singing'. Instead of going to church like most of the village he wandered out across the fields to the headland again, looked down on the cove to see that the boats were still safe – this salved his conscience and made him feel busy. The waves were strong, rose and curled, crashed onto the shingle and rattled the pebbles as they receded to gather again for the next onslaught. The little boats lay tranquil above the beach, high on the shingle bank. He felt the spray and blow wet on his face – the wind had risen since he and Jo had come to look at the boats earlier in the evening. The sea was wild and the roar of the surf deafened him. He was about to turn his back on the sea when there was a great flash across the water. 'There's a boat out there' he cried – 'My God they'll be drowned!' They're coming in – they'll run aground – My God they waves 'll smash um.' He turned and hurried back the way he had come. Carefully climbing the slippery path which rose in a series of steep ledges to the fields above, dense undergrowth of gorse and sloe on either side – he clutched at these with his bare hands and the thorns and prickles drew blood. His clumsy boots slipped and slithered over the wet mud and stones. The steepness of the path made him labour for breath. There was the taste of blood in his mouth – breathless he reached the field above. He stopped to look back – Yes there she was a great ship floundering among the waves – the sails torn and flapping in the wind. He could see her quite plain now. There must be someone on board who knew the cove for he felt sure she was trying to fight her way round to the quiet inlet of Horseshoe Cove. He could hear men shouting, a woman screamed. The moon went behind a bank of cloud. Losing sight of her he turned and hurried on.

The breath in his chest hurt him and his legs felt numb as in some awful dream he forced them forward against their will, his boots kept sticking fast in the mud and hurt him. He made for the barn at Bell Farm – he would toll the bell. The whole village would hear and come running, and Parson must nigh have finished by now and Jo would be out of church. He could see the barn before him by the fitful light of the moon and gathered his strength to cross the last field. Reaching the barn at last he struggled with the great bar that held the double doors, at last he slipped the bolt, the great doors creaked apart – it was pitch dark inside and he had to think which side the ladder was. He stumbled over a bit of old chain, fell against a hen roost clutching at its sides which tore and scratched his fingers. The hens took fright, flew off their perches cackling and setting up a din. He felt for the ladder which led to the loft above where the bell was hanging, finding it at last he climbed carefully, slowly, a slip now could mean death to all those aboard who he as trying to save. He must reach the bell and give the alarm. Reaching the top of the ladder he felt the floor of the loft above him – he drew himself up, and leant forward on to his chest as he raised his legs to the platform rolled over and lay for a moment exhausted. Then gathering his strength got painfully to his feet and cautiously felt his way to the bell pull, he knew it well but it was very dark – there! He felt it brush his shoulder – where was it – he spread his hands in feverish haste, his fingers found and held it, closed about the rope. He shut his eyes in the dark pulling with all his might, slowly the rope descended, then he heard the axle begin to move. The next instant the bell tolled out across the fields into the night, rent the air again and again in the silent village, tolled and tolled again. Ned sweated in the dark. The palms of his hands grew hot from the tope, still he tolled, how long he never knew.

After Mary and the Parson had left for the church, Martha Trethewey lay in the big four poster bed and dozed fitfully, the fire burnt low. For a time she had looked tenderly on the furnishings of her room. They had all come from her room at Bell Farm. This great bed with its now faded chintz hangings – the polished oak press in the corner that had held her trousseau – some of her linen was still in the bottom drawer and had never been disturbed. She was not an old woman – still in her 42nd year. She had been 26 when John Trethewey had courted and married her. Mary was their first child. She had been sickly after the birth and John had said they would wait for another. John! dear John!

How tender and gentle he had been with her, smoothing away her fears and cradling her in the warmth of his great arms – she could feel them now about her – strong and firm, reassuring, she turned on her side and sighed, nestled closer to him. She could hear his voice in her hair, close to her ear – murmuring – there! There! My dear 'tis no cause to be afrighted.

The bell tolled out rending the night with its clamour putting the wind to shame. Martha started up awake. The place beside her was empty – where was John? Who a moment before had been cradling her in his arms. She looked wildly round the room, it was almost dark. The candle had burnt low in its socket. The embers in the grate gave only a fitful glow – she threw back the covers and sprang to her feet all weakness now forgotten. There it was again 'The Bell – The Bell – The Bell' beating in her head. Scarce knowing what she was about – she ran to the closet in the corner and took out a brown homespun gown, drew it over her nightshift – drew on her thick woollen stockings and scarlet garters that Mary had given her last Christmas. Then taking her big cloak and pushing her feet into a pair of boots she made her way half stumbling down the stairs and out into the night. The cold wind smote her. She drew the cloak around her and crossed the yard to the street. She could see the church door standing wide the light streaming out. Still in a daze scarce knowing what she did or where she was going – impelled forward by strong forces beyond her control – she reached the church and went in – it was empty! The candles all ablaze, the Holy Vessels that had held the sacrament still on the altar. Martha went down the aisle, crossed herself and knelt at the altar rails praying she knew not what nor how long she knelt there.

Parson had almost finished the service when Ned had begun to toll the bell. He had given them his blessing and taken the vessels in his hand about to depart to the vestry. The air had been rent by the sudden clamour.

Jo tiptoeing to the belfry to ring the Christmas in had been frozen in his track. All heads were raised – the congregation rose as one man to its feet – Parson replaced the vessels on the altar and raised his hand to stay them. 'Good people' he cried, raising his voice till it echoed in the farthest corners. 'It is Christmas night – peace on earth, Goodwill towards men. Think not of yourselves this night but only of the deliverance from their sufferings of the people aboard this distressed ship, which God in his mercy has delivered into your hands' 'Amen' cried Jo and the congregation moving as one man in a mass for the door cried 'Amen' also.

Mary was in a panic – she got pushed and jostled at the door and could not get out – someone seized her arm – 'Come on' whispered Charlie in her ear. 'Leave us go round by the east door'. They backed out of the jostling crowd. Mary felt calm with Charlie's strong hand on her arm. They sped back down the aisle and across the Lady Chapel to the east door. It was not often used, the bolt was rusty, it took them a few minutes to dislodge it – she waited impatiently while Charlie worked it up and down. There – it went back with a jerk. Charlie put his foot against the door jamb and pulled, the little used door burst open. The full blast of the east wind blew the breath back down their throats and all the candles sputtered as it rushed in among them.

Once outside Charlie slammed the door again. They sped away into the night, slipping and slithering over wet grass and stones. Mary's dress caught on a splinter as they climbed a gate and tore leaving a bit behind. On and on across the fields they were nearing the headland now and the sea and wind was like thunder in their ears. People were running in all directions – voices crying and men shouting and cursing – Alf Jordan, Charlie's father was there, and here was Bill Mason panting up behind passing them, the great rope from the harvest wagon wound about his body, a pitch fork in his hand.

''Tis no manner of use going down to the cove' Charlie said, 'leave us cut across this 'ere field and come out near the headland – us can see more from there'. ''ess' said Mary and followed him. They ran like shadows to the headland. The moon shone out from behind a cloud – then they saw her! The little ship trying to keep herself from going aground in the swell. 'What is um' said Mary. 'Don't know' said Charlie, 'What ever 'a 'es – 'ee do know what 'ee's about – 'ee ant got no mind to come in 'ere – 'ess trying to round the point I believe – but 'tis dark when the moon goes in and 'ee can't see what 'ess about. 'Leave us go down to Horseshoe Cove Charlie and send a message', she said. 'We can't send no message' he cried ''Ow are us going to do that do 'ee think?' ''Ave 'ee got a tinder with 'ee' she shouted. 'Don't know' came the answer – 'Do 'ee feel in your pockets and be quick about 'un!' While Charlie felt in the capacious pockets of his great coat, Mary ran behind a bush, hitched up her skirt and started to untie her white cambric petticoat. 'Whatever are 'ee a doing of' cried Charlie, fishing out his tinder box and flint. 'I be going to set me petticoat alight' came the reply. 'We'll burn 'um on the cliff above the cove and if there be a man aboard who do know this coast 'ee'll see 'is way to get her in to shelter'. 'The tide is high and 'ee could berth un up against they fishing steps out in the cove.' ''Ess', said Charlie. 'Come on', he grabbed the petticoat slipping down the steep grass slope, till they were just above the little Horseshoe Cove, it lay with its back to the wind – it was quiet down there and the water was still. 'Quick' said Mary, 'Strike the tinder'. They bent together striving and fumbling – there was a spark – Mary pushed the petticoat nearer and it burst into flames. Charlie seized a furze branch broken off by the wind, caught up the flaming petticoat and waved it wildly in the air. A shout went up from the cove – there was an answering cry from the ship – she rose and fell and wallowed. Then slowly the sails filled out – the wind caught her full, carried her over the crest of the wave and out to sea a little way – then they lost sight of her, as the moon changed clouds they saw her again – she was level with the point clear of the rocks. If she kept course a little longer she could come about into the wind from the far side and drift into the cove on the incoming tide.

Mary held Charlie's hand tightly, the little ship battled on now in view now lost to sight – she prayed, her eyes tight shut – dreading to hear the crash if the little ship failed to make it round the point. Charlie put his arms round her and held her close – brushed his lips against her hair. "Tis alright my love, 'Tis alright my love', he repeated over and over again. She could hear his heart beating as she buried her face in his shoulder not daring to look. There was a sickening crash, instantly drowned by the thunder of the waves. 'Ah!' shouted Charlie. 'What is it' she cried, raising her head and turning round. "Tis a great wave 'ave smashed 'er mast'. The people on board could be heard now and again above the wind and surf shouting and crying to each other.

Charlie clutched Mary now with one arm and waved the other wildly in the air '"Er's going to make it. 'Er's going to make it' he cried. A great wave lifted her clear of the rocks on the point – she surged forward beyond the cove – then swung round into the wind all sails flapping, her broken mast trailing in the water. Like a duck with a broken wing, slowly she began to drift into the cove on the still rising tide – like a giant toy, washed up with the driftwood.

The headland was seething with people come round from the big cove. Down they went – wading into the water – to help bring her in and make fast – to help the exhausted crew and any others that were aboard.

Mary felt sick and weak – ''Tis alright me dear' comforted Charlie. 'They'm safe now. They'm coming in proper like no more than a duck upon a pond'. Mary looked, it was true, the little ship was coming in.

Charlie held her close once more – he pushed the hood back from her face and turned it up – then very gently he kissed her full on the lips. Mary surrendered herself to his arms and his strength became hers.

Mary was the first to recover herself. 'Leave us go 'ome and put the kettle on', she said. 'They'll need plenty of hot water and fire to dry their clothes. I reckon there's many a cottage will shelter a stranger this Christmas night', she said. 'Ess' said Charlie and taking her by the arm drew her away up the slope and over the fields to the village.

Mary and Charlie entered the warmth of the old kitchen. 'Do 'ee rake the embers together', she told him. 'Make up a great fire and put the kettle on while I run upstairs to see if Mother be alright'.

Mounting the stairs Mary became aware for the first time of her wet gown which clung to her legs since she had taken off her petticoat – but it was no time for that she thought, and forgot it again.

Martha's room was in darkness. The candle had burnt out, the fire was all but dead. 'Mother!' she said. 'Mother!' There was no answer. Panic seized her. 'Mother!' she called at the top of her voice. She felt her way round the room falling over things as she went – at last she felt the old press, pulled open the top drawer her fingers closed upon a candle. She stumbled back towards the red glow of the fire, reached for a taper in a pot beside the hearth and coaxed the ash and taper to a flame. Her hands shook as she lit the candle, the wick spluttered as the flame sprang up flooding the room with light. Mary seized the candle spilling the wax and crossed to the bed holding it above her head the better to see.

The bed was empty – the clothes flung back as if in a hurry – 'Mother!' she called, 'Mother'. There was only silence from the great bed and shuttered room. It was warm and stuffy after the wind on the headland. Mary put her hand to her throat as tho' she were choking, panic seized her again. She flew down the stairs, the candle held high, the hot wax spilling on her hand as she went. 'Charlie, she'm gone', she shouted. 'She ain't there – me mother b'aint in 'er bed!' 'Where ever is she to en?' he said 'I dunno! I dunno!' Together they ran to the parlour and back, all was dark and still – only the newly kindled fire on the hearth blazed and crackled. ''Ave she gone to the village' said Charlie. 'Maybe she'm gone to the church – come on leave us look for her'. Out into the night they went and over to the church as fast as their feet could carry them. The light still streamed out from the door and windows – people were returning from the cove shouting and calling to one another. Strangers amongst them were wet and dejected. Those with people to care for made for their homes. The rest made for the church. Mary and Charlie hurried to get there first. In at the open door – Mary stood transfixed! There on the altar steps stood her mother, her white night shift showing below her homespun gown – her great winter cloak about her shoulders. The hood thrown back her hair all in disorder. All trace of weakness had left her – she stood, fine and fearless expecting Mary knew not what!

There was a commotion in the porch behind her – folks were pushed in from without and stood aside, she moved back with Charlie to make way – her heart was beating wildly, she clutched at Charlie's arm, he squeezed her to him.

Jo and Ned Semmens and Alf Jordan came slowly in shuffling their feet as with a heavy burden and Mary saw borne amongst them the bent figure of a man. His clothes were dripping wet his hands hung limp – his face was spattered with blood, a blood soaked handkerchief was tied about his head. Carefully they carried him down the aisle and put him down by the altar steps. Martha stood like one in a trance, her eyes wild and dilated. Then 'John!' she said, scarcely above a whisper. 'John!' she cried. 'My John!' All the life flooding back into her face. She knelt beside him, took the big cold hands in hers and chafed them – rocking to and fro and murmuring as she did so. Her tears fell unashamedly on to his already wet face where the salt was stiffening his beard.

Parson was there pushing his way through – the crowd closed in and Mary felt faint, only Charlie's stalwart arm prevented her from falling.

A voice said "Tis John Trethewey! Come 'ome and no mistake'. The crowd took up the name and passed it from lip to lip. 'John Trethewey, John Trethewey'

Mary leapt forward as if she had been hit – fought her way thro' the crowd to the altar steps. There was Martha cradling her father's head in her lap and crying over him. Removing the handkerchief from his brow to reveal a gaping wound, which she gently wiped as she murmured to him.

Mary knelt beside her and took his hand – John stirred in his wife's arms – the colour returned a little to his face and he opened his eyes – his gaze rested on Martha. Then he turned his head a little and looked at Mary – his child.

Parson seeing he was about to faint again, fetched the silver cup from the altar held it high and blessed it again. Then he knelt beside John and slipping his free arm under his head raised it a little saying as he did so 'the blood of Christ which was shed for you – do this in remembrance of me'. Then he held the cup to John's stiff lips and helped him to swallow two or three sips of wine. John opened his eyes again and regarded the Parson.

'Sanctuary' he said in a hoarse whisper. 'Amen' said the Parson.

Jo Semmens went unnoticed to the belfry – seized the bell rope and began to pull. The bell rang out into the stormy night. The little crowd that remains were suddenly galvanised into action. They turned to each other with smiles and greetings. Jo and Ned helped by Alf Jordan gently took John from Martha's arms, raised him up and bore him away to the Rectory.

Mary and Charlie put their arms about Martha and led her from the church. Those who remained moved back to let them pass. A voice was raised 'A Merry Christmas to 'ee'. 'A Merry Christmas, A Merry Christmas', the joyous cry was taken up and passed from one to another.

'A Merry Christmas, A Merry Christmas' echoed round the vaulted roof.

While the bells rang out.